SUBURBAN HIGH

TALEN WILLIAMS

Illustration credit: Bryce Tweedale

Contents

PRELUDE

A BRIGHT WHITE LIGHT ENVELOPED the entire area. There were sounds slowly fading in and out, but they were, for now, faint and indescribable. Slowly but surely, the light faded and revealed scenery that the boy had only seen before on television shows. The sights of curtains, bedpans, and such became familiar to him, as well as the sounds. Above all, he heard a constant beeping sound. The boy slowly raised himself and immediately looked to his left to see a heartbeat monitor and the wires that connected it to his chest. He came to the realization that he was in a hospital bed.

The boy wasn't sure at first how he had gotten there. There wasn't anyone else in the room to ask the question, no doctors or nurses, no patient in the bed next to his, and, surprisingly, no sign of his parents, who he was sure would be at his bedside. Regardless, he wouldn't have asked anyone out loud, as he wasn't one to talk to people he didn't know. But it didn't matter; it all came back to him as he attempted to raise himself further to get out of the bed. A brief yet sharp sensation of pain came to the boy on the back of his neck. He took his left hand to caress the afflicted area when familiar sounds of arguing, swearing, screaming, and a loud honking rang in his head.

Immediately, the memory of the events leading up to this moment came back to the boy. He did his best to disregard the pain and leapt out of bed. He didn't call for anyone to let them know he was now conscious. Then again, he rarely showed concern for his well-being, so he didn't really care how long he'd been unconscious. He rushed out of the room and down the hallway of the hospital, looking at the signs on each door and quickly reading the names of the patients who were stationed in each room.

But each one that he passed didn't reveal the name he was looking for, causing the boy to become more frantic. The boy eventually stopped at the end of the hall at the nurses' station, panting and sweating, but more from the anxiety than the running. Before the nurse at the station could even form the words to call for a doctor in response to the boy's awakening, he screamed out the name of a girl and followed up by asking of her whereabouts.

The boy had gained the attention of nearby doctors and nurses, who nodded to the nurse at the station, hence her refusal to answer the question. They moved in closer to surround him in an attempt to calm him down. One doctor even reached in his pocket for a needle of what could be assumed to be a sedative. The boy noticed the mob of medical staff closing in on him and ran directly through them. His relatively small size worked to his advantage as he slipped through two doctors. He ran back down the hallway to a doorway leading to a flight of stairs. Still in a panicked state, the boy was now being pursued by members of the medical staff, including members of hospital security who had been notified of his "escape."

Closing in on him, the security patrol chased the boy from both the bottom and top flight of stairs. He only made it down two floors. With no other options available to him, he exited the stairwell on the floor he was currently on. He noticed an unoccupied elevator to the left of him and ran towards it. As he neared the elevator, he glanced at a window of a hospital room and saw several adult figures standing around a hospital bed, accompanied by a doctor and a nurse. It was at that moment that time seemed to slow down. The boy could now only hear his heartbeat at the pulse and rate similar to when something dramatic happened on one of his favorite TV shows.

Two of those figures belonged to his parents, who both stood over the hospital bed in a somber manner. Across from them was a couple. The woman turned her head slightly away from the bed, and began crying heavily upon the shoulder of the man at her side. It was only slightly, but the boy also recognized the face of the crying woman. It was the girl's mother, the girl who he was looking for.

The boy pushed the room door open in a dramatic manner that gained the attention of everyone save for the crying mother. Even so, there was only one sound that filled the room, the beeping sound that the boy had himself awoken to. Though the pitch was somewhat similar, this beeping sound came in the form of a flatter, more constant tone. The boy nervously walked toward the bed. The mourning couple separated themselves from their embrace to allow him to pass.

There, the boy saw her lying in that bed peacefully, her eyes closed, not making a movement, sound, or breath. And there he stood, nearly as motionless as she. The anxiousness that had filled the boy a moment ago was gone, along with any other emotion. As it was earlier, there was silence. The boy could not even hear the drops of the tears as they ran down his face and onto the floor, not even the footsteps of his earlier pursuers as they rushed into the room, not even the adults who attempted to comfort him. Shortly after the silence, the light that had enveloped his entire vision earlier returned. At that moment, the boy who wanted to see this girl, if only one more time, couldn't see anything at all.

Moments went by. The boy stood by himself, still surrounded entirely by white, until a stern voice called out to him.

"William," the voice beckoned, barely audible. "William," the voice called out again, now both louder and clearer than before. "William!" the voice shouted even louder.

The boy could now put a face to the voice that called his name.

Chapter One

Monday, August 23, 1999

The eyes of fourteen-year-old William Moon sprung open as his father shouted his name from the driver's seat. In response, Will quickly lifted his head from his right hand, which had been propping it up. Will then looked to his father with attentiveness, as the patriarch of the Moon family attempted to weave through Monday morning traffic, giving him a condensed version of one of his infamous lectures at the same time.

"Listen up, boy. Now, your momma wants you to go to this school and make all kinds of friends. She wants you to get involved in activities and have new experiences. She wants you to have moments that you'll remember all your life."

"Did she really say all that?" Will asked. "Sounds more like something out of one of those self-help books she's been reading."

"It don't matter," answered Will's dad. "What *does* matter is what I want. And what I want is not to be getting any phone calls from the school. Now, I busted my ass for years, and I finally got a decent paying job. Enough money to put us in that nice house in that fancy neighborhood. And I don't wanna lose it 'cuz I gotta take time off to come down to talk to your teachers 'cuz you don't wanna act right. I mean, you like that nice big house we got now, right? You like having a room to yourself, right? You like living in that neighborhood where the street lights work and the pizza man actually delivers? And you can walk around in shoes that cost more than fifty dollars and not have to worry about them getting stolen right from up off your feet? You want all that to go away?"

As he normally did, Will's dad prattled on louder and faster and seemingly with no intention of ever stopping his lecture. Fortunately for Will, the two had reached their destination, a vehicle drop off spot near the front quad of what appeared to be an above-average-looking high school.

The car came to a stop, and Will attempted to get out. But when he reached for the door, Will's dad sighed, signaling the continuation of his speech. Cars behind his honked loudly, and their drivers yelled at him to move up. Will didn't think his dad heard the honking, or if he did, it wasn't going to keep him from finishing what he had to say, regardless.

"You don't wanna make friends or whatever? Fine then. Just keep your mouth shut and your eyes open. You tracking?" he asked, harking back to his military days.

"Yes," William responded softly.

"What was that?" his dad asked somewhat intimidatingly.

"YES, SIR!" Will exclaimed as loud as he could, yet still very quietly and somewhat sarcastically.

"Good. Now get out the car, boy, you holdin' up traffic."

Will went for the door again, but paused briefly to ensure his father didn't have anything else to say. He gave a quick glance to his dad, who responded with a dismissive hand motion. He exited the black Isuzu Rodeo, which quickly drove off of the lot.

Will stared at the school in front of him for a moment. It kind of resembled one of those schools that set the scene of one of the recently released "teen" movies: a prep school rented out by the studio during the summer to give viewers the impression that there were hundreds of students attending, although the movie only focused on seven of them at most. Within his line of vision in any general direction, Will saw several students. Most, if not all, were Caucasian, roaming the campus in both anticipation and anxiousness for the first day of school. However, what caught Will's attention the most was the massive statue of the historic figure from which the school derived its name, George Washington.

Standing as proud and patriotic as the history books portrayed him to be, Washington looked towards the skies with an eagle perched on his right arm. A plaque was placed on the pedestal of the statue. A shining shade of gold at first, the plaque, like the statue itself, definitely showed its decades of wear and tear.

Despite his generally uninterested nature, Will walked with his hands in the pockets of his navy blue hoodie toward the statue of Washington to read the words on the plaque. With his hands still in his pockets, he squinted and tilted his head to the side as he tried to make out as many of the fading words as he could. "...Virtuous…youth…fail?" he read as those were the only words he could decipher from the old text. "What the hell does that even mean?" Will asked himself. Then, the voice of a young female was heard:

"The best means of forming a manly, virtuous, and happy people will be found in the right education of youth. Without this foundation, every other means, in my opinion, must fail."

Will turned his head to the right to see a girl taller than he, with a skin complexion much darker than his own and a single afro puff that dwarfed his short top fade in comparison tied in a black and white striped headband. The girl wore little makeup, but Will could easily assume that she could garner attention with her large hoop earrings, similar to those worn by the ladies who frequented the beauty shop his mother used to go to—especially—those who loved to go on about how they "didn't need no man!"

"Is that what that's supposed to say?" Will asked the girl.

"Mm-hmm," she replied, nodding her head. "They asked about that quote on an AP History exam I had to take last year. Of course, it's a little bit out of its time. Don't you think? I mean, back then women, and especially our ancestors, didn't have much access to the education he claimed would make us virtuous and happy. Shoot, we didn't even have that education fifty years ago when this school was founded."

"Sooo…?" Will asked blankly.

"So," she replied, "now that we *do* have access to this education, we have a responsibility to take full advantage of it!" The girl spoke passionately. "Not just for ourselves, but for our ancestors who didn't have this, and our brothers and sisters who still don't!"

Will continued his blank, confused stare at the girl who had started to bear a resemblance to one of the "soul sisters" on some of his parents' old records.

"I'm Krystal, by the way. A sophomore," Krystal said. She extended her hand out to Will, looking for a handshake. "And you are?"

Will kept his hands still in his pockets. "I'm…" he paused briefly and then continued nervously, "gonna be late for homeroom." Will walked quickly away from Krystal and towards the campus.

Moments later, as Will walked through the campus, passing the building that housed the cafeteria, the first bell of the day rang. Students began walking in every direction towards their classes. Will, however, pulled out a wrinkled piece of paper from his pocket. It was his class schedule, detailing the names of the courses his parents had registered him for, along with what periods these classes were for and where they were located. The top of that list read, "Homeroom - J. Pierce - 8:15 AM - E108." Will had about ten minutes to locate the E Building, a task that proved difficult as the many connected buildings that made up the main campus did not have a clear indication as to which one was which. Will put the schedule, now in a worse state than before, back into his jeans pocket and reached again into the pockets of his hoodie.

He pulled out a pair of earbud headphones, took a CD player out of his pocket, turned it on, and immediately turned to track seven. He and his cousin had burned the CD a month before from random songs downloaded off Napster's popular songs list. Track seven, in particular, had become a favorite of his. Although, he didn't share it with anyone – especially his parents, who triple-checked to ensure his every album purchase came from Wal-Mart, where only the clean versions of albums were sold, or his younger brother, who deemed himself "too black to listen to rock music."

The song was titled "Stinkfist" by the band Tool. About a month ago, Will had logged on to the internet at a local library with the purpose of finding the lyrics to the song. He came across a music discussion message board that posted said lyrics, but, more interestingly, it had a discussion comprised of more than a hundred posts over the meaning of said lyrics. Regardless of the lyrics' true meaning, Will interpreted them, and the song as a whole, in only one way. Before he left the house, Will's mother had assured him that he would remember the next four years for the rest of his life, as if they were the scenes of his favorite movie. If this were truly the case, then this song would serve as its opening theme. What kind of movie these next four years would turn out to be, however, remained to be seen.

The song played as Will navigated through the connected buildings. He hoped he'd be in the E building soon if he wasn't already, not oblivious to the irony that homeroom was the only class he had assigned in that building. He only knew that the room had to be on the first floor of the building because of the number 108, so he didn't bother traversing any of the many staircases in the buildings he walked through. Of course, he could've asked any of the many people he came across in his search for directions, but he didn't want to pause the song. On top of that, he wasn't feeling very talkative, either. So instead, he chose to walk past the security guard randomly patting down students, past the tall athletic boy wearing the green and gold letterman jacket who was busy making out with his cheerleader girlfriend, past the adult in the important looking dress skirt shouting commands at students walking by who would definitely tell him to take out his headphones if he approached her, and past the janitor who looked at the youth with eyes of utter disgust and disappointment. Will continued to walk through the halls, surrounded by the mass of tall green lockers, until the last words of the song were sung and the instrumental faded out. The tardy bell rang. Still not even sure what building he was in, Will uttered underneath his breath, "Crap."

A chime sounded from a nearby intercom: "Good morning, students, faculty, and staff of Washington High School. This is Principal Caine speaking. I'd like to welcome all of you to a new school year. Now, I know you all cannot wait to start learning, so I'll be brief. I want to remind everyone of our new school security measures. Students can be subject to searches at any given time and must cooperate with security officers or face disciplinary action. This includes pat-downs and metal detector searches. Additionally, if probable cause calls for it, students must submit to a urinalysis. Also, don't forget to show off your school spirit by wearing green and gold this week to wish our boys luck on the field this football season! Now then, let's have both a fun and fulfilling year full of educational experience!"

Another chime sounded from the intercom.

About eight minutes later, Will finally made his way to the E building where his homeroom class was. All that remained was to find room number 108. Will, unfortunately, came into the E building from the rear entrance, so he found himself staring at doors labeled 129 and 130. Room 108 would be down the hall quite a way. So, he started walking down the hall. He finally reached his destination. He took the earbuds out and turned off his CD player. The CD was set into a shuffle-play order, and Will didn't pay attention to what song played next. He looked down at the silver doorknob connected to the wooden door, but before he opened it, he let out a sigh.

Will didn't think any of the twenty-nine other students in the classroom gave much thought about him when he walked into homeroom. Of course, they looked up from their desks or whatever else commanded their attention at the time, but they gave one glance at him, who, after arriving ten minutes late, was technically the "new kid." Shortly afterward, having already passed their silent judgements on Will, the students went back to what they were doing besides paying attention to the teacher. They knew he wasn't anyone who was going to be considered "important."

The teacher, who was interrupted by Will's sudden entrance, also glanced at him. His judgment, however, wasn't as silent, but it was brief. "Oh great. Another one," he groaned, shaking his head and taking off his glasses to rub his eyes.

The teacher, James Pierce, stood at his desk at the front of the classroom with a tired look in his eyes. Here stood a man about in his mid-forties, with grey streaks intertwining in his auburn hair. His short mustache and goatee were similar in color, auburn mixed with gray. His beard, mostly composed of stubble, was unkempt and covered a good portion of the sides of his face. Will's first impression of Pierce was that of a man who has either given up altogether, or is living one day at a time with no significant goal, waiting for the inevitable end.

With one hand gripping a half-empty mug of coffee that read "#1 Teacher," Pierce spoke to Will now directly. "I'm going to assume that you're Moon."

Will nodded.

"Well, what are you waiting for Mr. Moon, an invitation?" He pointed in the direction of the desks. "Grab some wood, and be quick about it."

Will came to the conclusion that his options in who he was going to be sitting next to for the next year were severely limited. Of the thirty desks, which seemed like far too many for the small room, only one was empty. It didn't matter to Will, though. He wasn't too enthused about getting to know either of the other students on either side of him. Will forced his way to the back of the classroom as best he could, ignoring the few silent snickers of some of his classmates as he passed them. This was ideal for Will. The further back in the classroom he was, the less chance he had for being called upon for anything, or at least that was what he believed anyway.

The silence that filled the room as Will walked towards his seat was broken, and Mr. Pierce continued his lecture. "Now, before that interruption, I was saying that the student handbooks on your desks are yours to keep. It would behoove you to…you know…actually open it and read it. There's some pretty interesting things in there on tardiness, among other things. Now, I know some of you will read the thing word for word, cover to cover. Some of you may not even pay it any mind after I finish what I have to say. But regardless, each of you will refer to the very last page and sign it, confirming that you *will* follow the rules outlined in the handbook and that you accept the punishment that goes with violating those rules."

Will looked down on his desk and saw the book, about fifty-plus pages in length and bound in a green and athletic gold hardcover. Of the two groups Pierce mentioned regarding the handbook, Will would definitely be in the latter as he flipped directly to the last page and signed on the dotted line at the bottom of the page. Well, it was more like a scribbled line than a legitimate signature. Will had seen no need or use for cursive writing past the third grade. He closed the handbook immediately after his half-hearted signature. For all he knew or cared, there could have been a clause in there that allowed the school to sell the students to science or, even worse, market research.

Mr. Pierce was still going on about rules and guidelines. His speech seemed memorized, as if he'd given it many, many times before, as if it was as familiar to him as "The Pledge of Allegiance" or "The Lord's Prayer." The students were just as interested in hearing his spiel as he was in giving it, which was to say, not at all. One was reading an issue of a fashion magazine. Two were gossiping with each other. One passed a note to another, and so on and so forth.

Then, there was the student who sat next to Will. He, like every other student and the teacher, was Caucasian with somewhat-tanned skin. However, that was where the similarities ended. This "character," as Will would soon refer to him, wore a black sideways cap on top of a white du-rag covering his ginger red hair. Around his neck was a sterling silver necklace with medium-length links and a sterling silver dog tag necklace that went almost completely down his black Fubu jersey, separating the gold 0 and 5 in the middle of the shirt. His baggy navy jeans were only halfway covered up by his desk, but his brown Lugz boots stood out, the right one completely taking up that portion of the classroom floor. Will would have never made these observations, or at least never spoken on them; he would have never paid this "character" any mind at all throughout the year. But it was the "character" who made the first statement in a short conversation that taught Will more about him than he'd ever want to know.

"Say, man. You ain't from 'round here, are you? Where you from?" the classmate asked.

"Salem," Will responded, not sure why.

"Say word, son, for real? Salem? The SALEM?"

"Yeah. Why?"

The classmate leaned back in his desk as he used one of his hand to cover his mouth in both amazement and disbelief. "YOOOO!" he exclaimed. "That's dope! I heard that place was one of the hardest hoods out there! So yo, you roll with the Twenties?" He was referencing a notorious street gang based out of Will's previous town. Before Will could respond, his classmate continued, "Nah, that's Blood gang. I see you rocking that blue; you probably ran with them Lost Boys." This was a reference to a rival gang that fought for territory in the Salem area.

Will still didn't answer immediately. He took note of his classmate's obviously forced slang speech. He was clearly new at this.

"I didn't roll with any gang," Will finally responded.

"Oh I see," said the classmate. "You rode solo. That's real dope, that's what I do. Do my own dirt, put in my own work, split my cheddar with nah 'nother person, know what I'm sayin'?"

Will gave the classmate a stern yet confused look, "I have no idea what you're saying."

"Say, homie, it's cool 'cuz you in my hood now, feel me? What's your name, homie?"

"William. Everybody just calls me Will."

"Okay, Will," the classmate said. "I'm Rob. But everybody 'round here calls me 'Big Rob Dawg' or 'Rob 'em Up' or…"

"Mr. Stanley!" Pierce shouted.

"Huh?" Rob replied, shifting his view from Will to the front of the class. "What's up?"

"Well, since you're in such a talkative mood, Mr. Stanley, perhaps you can tell us what the student handbook says about vandalism of campus property."

Rob answered, "It's just Rob, man. None of that 'Mr. Stanley' stuff. And nah, I can't tell you. I ain't read that part yet."

Pierce smirked sarcastically. "Hmph, well then, maybe your new friend, Mr. Moon, can tell us. Or the both of you can get further acquainted in detention after school today."

Will gave Rob an angry look. He, too, looked towards the rest of the class. "Ummm," Will replied quietly, "don't do it?"

Pierce didn't respond immediately. He stared at the two, took a brief sip from his coffee mug, and then placed it down on his desk. "Yes. Don't do it. Not the exact answer I was looking for, but still a correct answer nonetheless. Keep those words in mind, class, don't do it. Let those words swirl in your mind and remain there. Any time you have to pause for even a second to ask yourself if what you're about to do is a good idea, heed Mr. Moon's words. Don't. Do. It."

The other students turned around to look at Will. Their looks varied, but Will only seemed to notice the few who gave him disapproving scowls. Previously, Will had believed that their opinion of him was that of indifference. Now it had to be one of utter contempt. Although it was faint, as it came from the front of the classroom, Will could hear one student suck their teeth and proclaim him a "suck up."

Rob whispered to Will, "Good lookin' out, homie."

The other students turned back around in their seats. Rob extended his fist out to Will looking for a fist bump. Will, his hands still at his side, let out another sigh, similar to the one he gave before he opened the classroom door. "No problem… homie."

Chapter Two

The remainder of the morning was uneventful for William, much to his approval. There were three class periods after homeroom, each in different buildings: one in the C building, the next in the G building in the west-most end of the school, and the final in the A building in the front of the school near the administration building. Though Will still hadn't become acquainted with the layout of the buildings, his pace as he walked from classroom to classroom was a bit faster. He didn't want to be late for another class. The last thing he wanted was to be the center of attention again, for any reason, even if only for a moment. Again, he could have asked any of the various individuals crowding the halls in between periods for directions, but he didn't.

With his earbuds in and his CD player playing tracks in random order, Will navigated through the halls. He managed to find himself in the back of the classrooms for each of the classes, and, luckily, he sat next to students who weren't as eager to make conversation with him as Rob had been. During third period, Mrs. Fleming, a freshman English teacher, called on Will to answer a question about something related to literature comprehension. Will had no desire to give the answer, even if he knew what it was. So instead he shrugged his shoulders without a sound.

Ignoring his peers, and being ignored by them, proved easier in time during and between classes, but Will found being alone during lunch impossible now. He still wasn't familiar with the layout of the school, but this was to be expected; this was the first day of school. It would be some time before he would be completely familiar with the school's layout. So, even if there was somewhere he could be alone for the following forty-five minutes, he didn't know where it was. A thought did come into his mind, though.

Will remembered a Manga that he bought a year or so ago at the Base Exchange his parents visited on a weekly basis. They didn't sell too many of those, so he bought it out of sheer interest. This fairly obscure Manga, the title of which Will couldn't even remember, told the story of five teenagers who piloted giant robots, standard fare in the medium. When the team wasn't fighting aliens, monsters, other giant robots, or alien monsters IN giant robots, they lived normal lives as normal Japanese high school students. One of the members of the team of pilots, the pilot of the mech that was far more powerful than the others, and whose name Will had the hardest time pronouncing, was a shy girl who had no friends in school. She ate lunch alone all the time. She was known for taking her lunch and eating it in a toilet stall in the girls' bathroom.

Will wasn't about to go that far to isolate himself. A society that can afford to give giant robots to teenagers could definitely afford to have much cleaner toilets than the ones at Washington. On top of that, Will heard his stomach growling, even though the music was blaring through his earbuds. As usual, Will had skipped breakfast. He never bought into the "theory" that it was the most important meal of the day. In fact, he found breakfast to be overrated. So, Will had to at least walk through the cafeteria to the lunch line.

Will grabbed one of the green plastic trays, still slightly damp from the rinse cycle, and a plastic fork, knife and straw, bundled with a napkin in a plastic wrapper, and took his place in a line of students, sandwiched in between a taller girl who stalled the line as she decided what color gelatin she wanted, and a taller, muscular student in a varsity jacket. He was rushed along in the line as something that could probably constitute as food was hastily thrown on his tray by one of the lunch ladies. The only thing that Will recognized were the peas, some of which were more brown than they were green. At the end of the line, Will grabbed a carton of milk from the plastic container filled with ice. It was the last carton of chocolate milk.

"HEY!" a large athletic boy behind Will exclaimed in a burly voice, placing his giant hand on Will's shoulder.

Will took out one of his earbuds and turned his head to the side to address him. "Yeah?"

"Is that the last chocolate?"

Will didn't answer. Observing the boy's muscular build, giant size, and intimidating posture, he concluded that the easiest course of action would be to hand over the chocolate milk to him. So he did. Will didn't even like chocolate milk, or milk at all for that matter, but the only money he had was the ten dollars his parents had placed in his cafeteria account during school registration, so he couldn't get a soda from one of the machines. The boy grabbed the milk from Will's hand and showed his appreciation in a manner fitting those in his social circle. He shoved Will to the side and proceeded to the front of the line, shoving others smaller than he, meeting up with others bearing his physical resemblance.

"You're welcome?" Will muttered.

Will made it to the cashier at the end of the line and handed over his student ID card. The cashier swiped it through a card reader attached to the side of a computer monitor without so much as looking at the screen. She grabbed the printed receipt and put it randomly on Will's tray, her focus still on the line of students behind him and nothing else. "NEXT!" she yelled in a voice that clearly indicated she had smoked one too many cigarettes in her life.

Will walked away from the line and towards the tables. Without separating the receipt from the mush it was placed upon, Will glanced at it reading the words, "Remaining balance $7.60." Will was by no means a mathematician, but he knew that at this rate, by the end of the week, he'd be bringing a bag lunch to school and that he'd have to wake up earlier than he'd ever want to prepare it.

With tray in hand, Will stood and observed the cafeteria in search for an empty table. Right in front of him stood longer tables on both sides. Each of these "tables" was composed of three rectangular tables joined together. Each set of tables looked as if it could seat about ten to fifteen people.

One of these sets was occupied by athletes. From their physical stature, it was safe to say that most of them were members of the football team. There were the much larger guys who were probably part of the varsity team. And then, there were the smaller guys, who probably were on the JV squad. Of course, some of the varsity guys were picking on the JV members at the table. Will wasn't sure if this was some kind of initiation process or just the strong dominating the weak, like animals in the jungle. Will also caught a glimpse of the football player whom he had given his chocolate milk to in line. His teammates sitting around him laughed like a pack of hyenas as he squashed the carton of chocolate milk on his forehead. Will couldn't hear a word they were saying, but he was positive that there was nothing but praise being showered upon the milk-soaked athlete for his amazing display of physical prowess.

Unlike the cafeteria in Will's middle school, in which tables were filled in accordance to classes, the tables here were filled by members of particular social circles. On the other side of the table filled by the football players and other athletes was a table filled by older students – seniors, by the look of it. Will didn't get too much of a glance at them. He didn't want any of them looking back at him and wondering what his problem was. But what he did observe was that, other than gender, there wasn't much of a difference between the students that filled this table and the one next to it. Overall, they had nice hair and wore seemingly-expensive clothes, and the movement of their lips insinuated that they were having conversations about the most important things, like who's wearing what and who's dating who. Others were pre-occupied by their cell phones but would raise their heads when whatever conversation was being held began pertaining to them. The other two longer tables were occupied by a random assortment of students. There were still groups of students that sat together, but the groups were much smaller, leaving empty seats.

Will walked towards the other end of the cafeteria, near the entrance he came in from and the dish washing station where students were supposed to leave their trays when they were done. In this area, there were small, circular tables. Like the previous two larger tables, they were occupied by collected members of different social groups. It took some time, but Will was able to find a completely empty table in the middle of the area. With his tray high above his head, he squeezed through the occupied tables, constantly excusing himself and trying his hardest not to spill any of the contents of his tray onto himself or anyone else. After some time, he took his seat at the empty table. He placed his tray down on the table and took note of the disorganized mess that made it up now. Pieces of each food item mixed with each other made Will's lunch even more undesirable than before. With his fork, Will attempted to reorganize the food into something recognizable. For several minutes, he stared down at his tray. He didn't look up from it once until a voice called out to him.

"This seat free?" a boy asked Will.

Still down looking at his tray, Will responded, "Take it."

"Cool," said the boy.

Will thought for sure that the boy standing on the other side of the table across from him would take the chair and leave. Instead, the boy placed his tray, full of food and something wrapped in a bunch of napkins, down on the table. Then, he placed his red mesh backpack around the back of his seat and sat down. Will now looked up to see this boy who was now sitting at the same table he was.

The boy, who appeared to be a bit skinnier than Will, was wearing a black beanie, covering a small portion of his medium length, black hair. There were a few pimples on his face, but they were only noticeable if you looked at them hard enough. There was a bit of blackish peach fuzz on his chin and under his nose. He wore a black button-up shirt that was unbuttoned, revealing a red T-shirt with the words "Skunk Label" printed in white on top of two disconnected, black bars, one for each of the two words.

The boy unwrapped his fork from its plastic wrapping and started poking and jabbing at the food on his tray. "Aw, dude, what the hell is this stuff?" he asked.

Will pointed at the peas on the boy's tray with his fork in hand. "I think those may be peas."

"And I think I'll pass," he replied with a disgusted look as he pushed the tray to the side. "It's William, right?" he asked without provocation.

"People just call me Will," Will answered. "How'd you know?"

"I thought that was you, but I wasn't sure."

"Huh?" Will asked confused. He was positive he had never held a conversation with this individual whatsoever before now. "Do I know you?"

"Well, not personally. But, dude, we've got algebra with Patterson second period. Not surprised you didn't recognize me, though. You looked like you was in another world the whole time. I don't think had your head up once the whole time. Did you even see that super hot chick that sat in front of you?!"

Will didn't respond.

"Eh, never mind. I'm Nathan. Sometimes, people call me Nate for short."

Nathan didn't extend his hand out to Will for a handshake or any other gesture of greeting like Krystal or Rob had. It was safe to say his hand wasn't going to reach across the table as well as his voice did. "But, dude, that girl that sits in front of you? She is *too* fine! What curly blonde hair, those legs in that skirt and not to mention that sweet set of…"

Nathan could've gone on all lunch period about this particular girl, but Will felt inclined to interrupt. "What's in the napkins?" he asked, referring to the small object near Nathan wrapped in in the plain white napkins.

"OH CRAP! I FORGOT!" Nathan shouted. "She's gonna kill me, dude!" he said with a nervous smile on his face.

Will didn't ask Nathan who he was referring to, but he was sure it wasn't the girl Nathan had spent the last few minutes describing in adoration.

"I was supposed to give this muffin to Ashley. You haven't seen her anywhere in the cafeteria, have ya?"

Will shrugged his shoulders. He had no idea who Ashley was.

"You have no idea who I'm talking about do you?" Nathan asked.

Will shook his head silently.

"Well, she's about our size, more your height than mine. In fact, she's got the same brown skin as you, too, but I think you might be a bit darker. She's got a dark brown bobbed haircut that goes down to about halfway past her neck. A nice looking girl, modest, but for my tastes, she's lacking in the…"

Before Nathan could finish, Will interrupted. "Haven't seen anyone like that."

"Nah, I didn't think she'd be in the cafeteria. She asked me to bring her a muffin, but she didn't tell me where she'd be."

Nathan reached into his jeans pocket and pulled out a small, grey cellular phone. He looked down at the monochromatic screen and said, "Nope, not even a call or text message." Nathan started tapping away at the keys on the phone, saying the words aloud as he typed, "Where…are…you? I've…got…muffin." Nathan placed the phone on the table and stared at it, waiting for a response.

Meanwhile, Will grabbed the plain slice of white bread on his tray and, still feeling hungry, started eating it faster than he should have. He began to hiccup profusely. Nathan couldn't help but notice as Will's hiccups became louder and more frequent.

He also noticed that Will didn't have anything to drink to quell the hiccups.

"Here, dude, take this," he said, pushing his unopened carton of 2% milk over to Will.

"Thanks," Will said after a set of hiccups.

He attempted to open the carton, but to no avail. He took the straw that came with the fork and napkin in a plastic wrapper and jabbed it into the carton. He drank the entire carton of milk within seconds, curing his hiccups. "If she isn't in the cafeteria during lunchtime, where could she be?" Will asked. He wasn't actually curious about Ashley's whereabouts; he was still scouting places where he could be to himself during lunch.

"Hmm," Nathan answered reluctantly. "Not sure, dude. I'm not too familiar with the lay of the land yet. But, ya know, when we were in middle school, she'd duck out to the library during lunch. She'd be on one of the computers doing God-knows-what."

Just then, a vibration rocked the table, followed by a set of beeping noises. It came from Nathan's cell phone. Nathan picked it up and read the message on the screen. "In the library. Hurry up. So hungry!" Nathan looked back to Will. "Eh, the more things change, right?" With that, he stood up from his chair and put his backpack on. He then put his cellphone back in his pocket and grabbed the napkin-wrapped muffin. "Later, dude," Nathan said. He didn't push his chair back in, and he left his still-full tray on the side of the table.

Will was finally alone, and he assured himself that nobody else would be joining him at the table. Just then, students from several different tables in all areas of the cafeteria started getting up. With trays in hand, they walked towards the dishwashing area and formed a line to bus their trays in the assembly line that sent them to the back area.

Will took a look at the clock at the top of the wall directly in front of him above a series of soda machines. The clock read 1:20 p.m. In five minutes, the bell would ring for the next period. The line at the bussing station was getting larger. If Will joined it now, he'd be late for his next class, for sure. So he got up from his seat, put back on his earbuds and turned on his CD player, put back on his solid black backpack, and proceeded to exit the cafeteria. He left his tray on the table just as Nathan did before.

Chapter Three

Two more class periods stood between the end of lunch and the end of the school day, and while the former of the two went off without a hitch, as for the latter not so much. Will sat in the back of his last period classroom, slouched over with his head on one of his hands, paying more attention to the clock than the teacher's lecture.

"A neurosurgeon, eh? That's a pretty lofty goal. But not one that can't be achieved. Okay then, Chelsea, take your seat." The teacher, Mr. Carlisle said to the class. "Okay then, let's hear from…" "Ah! William Moon."

Hearing his name, Will frantically shifted his attention from the clock on the side wall to the front where the young teacher was casually sitting on his desk rather than the chair that accompanied it. Will hadn't heard a word that was spoken during the entire class to this point, but he had already figured out what questions he was going to be asked. Behind Mr. Carlisle on the whiteboard read only one statement written in red marker:

"Today's Class: Who Are You?!" the "you" was underlined three times.

"Please stand up and tell the class a bit about yourself," Mr. Carlisle requested.

With no choice in the matter, Will rose from his chair, with his hands now placed back in his hoodie pockets, and saw the blank stares from the other twenty-eight students in the classroom. Their stares pierced through him like multiple spears going through the chest of a fallen warrior from ancient times. This was the first time, not just today, but in a long time, Will had to directly address a crowd of this size. To him, it was as if he was on trial and the utterance of one wrong word would send him straight to the electric chair.

"Um…" Will nervously began. "I'm Will. I moved here a few weeks ago from a town called Salem." He stood there, glassy-eyed, saying nothing else.

"And?" the teacher asked, hoping to squeeze more information out of Will. As if he was powered by a car engine, he threw a considerable amount of questions at Will. "What are your hobbies? What's your favorite subject? What do you want to do after you graduate? Do you want to go to college? What do you want to major in? You plan on getting married? Having kids? How many?"

Will had but one answer to all of the questions being torpedoed at him, "uh…"

Mr. Carlisle let out a tiny chuckle. A chuckle that some might've considered condescending if they thought about it hard enough. Will was just relieved that his interrogation was over.

He wasn't paying attention before, but he was positive that no student before him was hit with such a flurry of questions

"It's okay, William. I don't expect you to have all of the answers right here and now. But, students, these are just some of the questions you will have to find the answers to. You can take your seat now, Mr. Moon."

Without hesitation, Will sat back down. The optimistic teacher, who looked like he still believed that the children had bright futures and wasn't just at work to collect a paycheck rather than mold young minds, began to give a passionate speech.

"You know, you lot are lucky. We are heading into a brand new millennium. Technology and the innovations that come along with it are growing at a rapid pace. And you sitting in those desks right now will be the ones that spearhead our society in the 21st century. Decades from now, your names will be written in the history books your descendants will study from. It is up to each and everyone of you to decide what will be said about you in those books, just as the people you'll read about in your text did before you. So this history course won't be just about learning about the past, I'm hoping that you will also learn about yourselves so that when your grandchildren live in an utopian society, they'll know exactly why it was your actions that made it so. That is why I ask the question." He pointed at the words he wrote on the whiteboard. "WHO? ARE? YOU?!"

The bell rang after that. The students rose from their desks and emptied the classroom ten times faster than they entered it. "We'll begin with the unit on the forming of the colonies tomorrow. Start reading chapter one tonight," Mr. Carlisle exclaimed to the students as they left.

Will walked toward He was a few steps away from the classroom door when he was halted by Mr. Carlisle who grabbed his left shoulder. With his eyes closed and a smile on his face, Carlisle addressed Will, "Didn't mean to put on the spot like that, Moon. Just wanted to see if you were paying attention. You know what say about history. Those who fail to learn from it… well, you know the rest."

Will didn't respond, he just kept walking towards the door.

Will didn't go to his locker to put the textbooks he received away, they remained in his backpack. They were heavy, or they would have been, if they weren't old and outdated. The worn pages definitely lightened the burden on Will's back. He didn't want to spend another moment at Washington that he didn't have to. On top of that, his locker was back in the E building, where his homeroom class was, and there was no way he was traversing back there.

Will made his way to the west end of the campus, where he could see a series of yellow school buses parked behind one another in a single-file line. Even if he knew which bus would take him home, Will had had his fill of interacting with his peers for the day. Even being near them would have overwhelmed him at this point, so he made the brash decision to walk home. He had memorized the route his dad took from their house to the school in the morning. He also determined that it would take about twenty to thirty minutes to walk home.

With his hands in his pockets, yet again, Will walked between two of the buses towards the chain link fence that bordered the school along the main roads. He discovered that the school buses and the seniors with cars shared the same parking lot, as he had witnessed several of them conversing with each other around their cars. There were exits from the lot on both the east and west of Will's position; the west led toward the main road, and the east led back toward the front of the campus where he was dropped off this morning. He pushed on towards the west exit, despite it being further than the east.

As he walked, he began to turn on his CD player and put in the earbuds. He had placed the right earbud in his ear when suddenly he heard a large, roaring noise heading toward him. It was the sound of the engine of a Chevy Corvette driven by a senior at a speed that blatantly violated the 10 mph limit of the parking lot. As the cherry red, newish looking car whizzed past Will, the sound of the music coming from the right earbud was drowned out by the roar of the car's engine, combined with the generic pop-rock music blaring from its radio and the exclamation of "WOOOOO! SENIORS, BABY!" from the girl in the passenger seat followed by a series of honks from the car's horn by the driver. This triggered Will to jump a short height in the air in shock. After he recovered, Will caught his breath and then put in the left earbud.

The walk home was a peaceful endeavor for Will. During the last days of August, there was a nice, calming breeze in the air. Fall was definitely on its way. Though he was more of a fan of the blazing heat of summer days, Will welcomed the brisk warmth that this particular day was filled with. The sun was still high in the sky, but sunset would come in about an hour or so.

After leaving the campus, Will began walking on Chisholm Road, one of the major roads of the town of Ingram Park. It was also one the busiest as it connected to the major highway and housed several business and stores on both sides of the road. If school let out even thirty minutes later than it did, Will's walk home would be spent fighting heavy traffic from disgruntled employees desperate to get home.

No less than five minutes into his walk from school, Will came across Park Hills Mall, an impressive three-story building that dominated the left side of his vision for at least eight more minutes. He recalled his mother telling him how big the mall was from the inside when she went there to buy him clothes for school. Seeing it for the first time at this scale, Will was admittedly impressed by the structure, although he wouldn't show it.

If Will continued down Chisholm Road, the mall would dominate its left side for at least a few more minutes, but he had to cross onto Benbrook Street to get home. His walk was halted by a three-way intersection that was dictated by traffic lights. Chisholm was the dominant street, so the lights on its side remained green much longer than the light that would allow Will to cross.

Across the street was a small strip mall composed of varying businesses including a tattoo parlor, an insurance agency, and an authorized dealer of mobile phones and services. At the tail-end of the strip mall, closest to the sidewalk, was a convenience store with gas-filling stations at its front. The store was sparsely populated, but occupying the area near its entrance were a group of kids—four of them, to be exact. The kids looked to be about his age. They stood by the entrance, drinking drinks from the store chain's signature cups, much to the store clerk's objection and in defiance of the sign right next to them reading, "No Loitering."

Finally able to cross the street, Will walked on the sidewalk of the same store in the strip mall. He was able to get a closer look at the kids and confirmed that they were teenagers, but he was not sure if they were Washington students. Their attire was similar to Nathan's. Some wore caps, others wore beanies, and one of them was wearing black fingerless gloves. They were all wearing different-colored, short sleeved T-shirts with different phrases and brands on them, all of which were brief, the longest being only three words. With the exception of one, they were all wearing the same style of shoes, a pair of low cut shoes with varying colors that kind of matched the color of their shirts and tight fitting, black jeans. Along with their large soda cups, each of the kids had skateboards near them. The overall scene reminded Will of the groups of students that had occupied each of the tables in the cafeteria; most of the groups were composed of students that bore the same resemblance to each other in some way or the other.

Like Chisholm Road, Benbrook Road had sidewalks on both sides for pedestrians, but Benbrook Road also had specially-marked lanes on the street closest to the sidewalks that were designated for bicyclists. There were no businesses on Benbrook

Road, only residences. It was quieter on this road than Chisholm, so Will could actually hear the music coming from his earbuds. Will walked on the sidewalk for a few minutes until he came across a bridge over a brook that looked like it went on for miles.

After crossing the bridge, Will entered Benbrook Road's residential area. On Will's left side were a series of apartment complexes separated by fences, each made of different materials, which helped distinguish the amount of money it cost to live in each complex. On his right was a row of single story houses with trees that seemed tall enough to eclipse the sun between them. Regardless of their height, their overall structure differentiated them from one another.

Will continued to walk down Benbrook for a while. He saw small children playing, running around, as hyperactive as children can be. Past the apartments on the left side, there were avenues and cul-de-sacs that led to even more houses, but none of these would be the street that Will had to turn onto.

Eventually, the sun shown again. It was further down in the sky than it had been before, indicating that sundown was quickly approaching. Will had exited the Benbrook Road residential area and the tree line that canopied it and found himself at a busy four-way intersection. Across the street, Will would find his destination.

There it stood, Presley Place, an enormous residential subdivision sealed off by a wall made of grey bricks. Will crossed the street and made his way to the closed entrance gate. The gate could only be opened by entering the code on the keypad on the median between the entering and exiting lanes. Will thought he remembered the code, but when he typed it in, he was greeted with a sharp buzzing sound that could be heard even through the music coming from his earbuds. A few seconds later, he tried again, entering the same number combination, under the impression that he typed it incorrectly the first time. Another buzzing sound rang.

Now Will was stuck. "What's that code?" he asked himself as a SUV pulled up beside him. He moved out of the way of the keypad, allowing the driver, a disgruntled looking man in a charcoal grey suit, to enter the code. A different, more welcoming sound chimed from the keypad, and then the gate on Will's and the driver's side opened. The driver gave Will an apprehensive look, as if he thought Will was trying to break into the neighborhood. To further drive that suspicion, Will saw that the man was pulling out his cell phone as he drove past the open gate. He wondered if the man was calling the police on him for trespassing, but he had to put the inquiry on hold as the gate started to close, prompting him to walk swiftly past it behind the driver; he wasn't looking to experience another awkward moment like this one.

Presley Place was far more expansive on the inside than it looked on the outside. It was composed of several roads connected the main road, most of them ending in cul-de-sacs. There were both one- and two-story homes, each of varying colors and designs. On the outside, it appeared that each house was custom-built from the preferred design stylings of the homeowners themselves. There were a few houses with "For Sale" signs placed on freshly mowed lawns, leading to Will to believe that, in the end, the owners weren't too pleased with their own design tastes. Why else would anybody want to leave a suburban paradise like this? Especially one so well guarded by a neighborhood watch and patrolling members of the Ingram Park Police Department.

Surprisingly, Will didn't see as many kids playing outside here as he did on Benbrook Street. Most of the noise that drowned out Will's music was the barking of dogs that were being walked by housewives as they jogged in their tracksuits. There weren't as many trees either. Besides the gardens and yards that were tended to by residents or landscapers hired by residents, the flora of the land was replaced by hundred-plus thousand dollar homes.

Will walked down the main road of the subdivision, only a few minutes between him and his house. A school bus passed Will and stopped ahead near an intersection. A few students exited the bus. During its stop, Will recognized the numbers on the back of the bus: 119. It was one of the buses that was parked in the lot back at Washington, leading Will to believe that if he were to take the school bus, this would be the one.

In the middle of Presley Place was Penley Avenue. The very first house on the left side of Penley Avenue's west end was the Moon residence, a two-story house made of grey bricks that looked plain in design when compared to the other houses in the area. The grass was a bit taller than the lawns of the houses beside this one, an observation Will made followed by a groan. He knew that either his dad or the Presley Place Homeowners Association was going to make him mow the lawn over the weekend. Near the mailbox in the front of the house was a basketball hoop that stood about fifty inches tall. It was in fairly new condition. It had only been used twice by Will's dad and Will's brother DeMarcus since it was purchased a few weeks ago. It was also the only one that Will saw in the entire neighborhood. Parked in the driveway was the bright pink Hyundai Accent which belonged to his mother. She, along with everyone else in the family, dubbed it the "Pink Bunny," and despite Will's dad's numerous requests, she refused to sell it for a new car, claiming it still had at least good ten thousand miles left in it. Near the driveway and front door and below the large window panes was a small area sealed off by grey stones of varying size. Inside this area was mulch made of wood chips with store-bought plants of different colors planted in it.

Will walked up the driveway and onto the pavement that bridged the driveway to the front door. He stood under the arch that covered the front door, took off his earbuds, and placed them back in his hoodie pockets. He didn't have to turn off his CD player; the batteries had died minutes earlier. He reached in his jeans pocket for the house key that was attached to a keychain in the form of a cartoon character. He put the key into the door's keyhole, but before he turned the key to open the door, he let out yet another sigh, similar again to the one he gave before entering homeroom.

Chapter Four

"What in God's name is that smell?"

Will got a whiff of the pungent aroma that lofted from the kitchen to the living room and front door. He took a longer smell and concluded, "Mom's cooking, isn't she?"

"Yup," a voice from the living room replied. It came from DeMarcus, Will's younger brother. He was lounged on the brown sofa that covered a large portion of the width of the living room, watching the television. "Another recipe from those magazines she gets."

Still standing by the front door, which was covered in linoleum tile flooring, Will rolled his eyes and asked, "Why nutrition? She could've majored in something useful like, I don't know, underwater basket-weaving or something."

"SHH!" cried DeMarcus as he pointed to the television. "Jerry is about to tell Shaquana who her baby daddy is!"

Will took off his black sneakers. With both sneakers in one of his hands, he walked through the living room to the staircase between the living room and the kitchen. Halfway up the stairs, Will's mother called him from the kitchen.

"Is that you, William?"

"Yes, ma'am!" Will shouted.

She popped out from the kitchen and to the bottom of the stairs.

"Come back down here!" she said excitedly. "I want to hear about your first day!"

"I'll tell you about it at dinner. I got homework I gotta do," he replied.

"Wait!" DeMarcus chimed in. "Y'all get homework on the first day?! That's some ol' bull right there! Man, I ain't never goin' to high school!"

Will didn't answer DeMarcus. He just kept walking upstairs. His room was towards the back of the house. To get to it, he'd walk through the entertainment room past both his brother's and sister's bedrooms. Unlike their rooms, the door to Will's room was closed. Although there weren't any locks on the door, Will felt entitled to at least a little privacy.

He entered the room and closed the door behind him. He didn't turn on the light; there was still a bit of sunlight that gleamed through the hardly open blinds that covered the windows. He dropped his shoes on the floor and his backpack from his shoulders and noticed the bundle of clothes folded neatly on his full size bed, some of which still had on the tags from the stores they were purchased. On top of the bundle was a yellow Post-it note with writing that resembled his mother's handwriting. Will picked up the note and read it to himself. "I bought these clothes for a reason," the note read. "Good to know she retained that passive-aggressiveness from college," Will said to himself.

Will took the bundle of clothes and placed them on the brown mahogany dresser nearby, along with the CD player from his pockets. He then plopped down on the now-empty bed and sighed as he looked at the ceiling and the slowly rotating ceiling fan. Some time later, Will looked to the left and reached towards the bedside table. He opened the top drawer and grabbed a composition notebook. It was old, and it showed its age.

Will sat up on the side of the bed next to the table and opened the notebook to a specific page with no writing on it to pull out a photo that was in it. It was a worn out Polaroid photo. On the bottom white portion read the date the photo was taken, "6-12-1999." Will's fourteenth birthday. The photo itself was of Will, in a purple button-up shirt and blue jeans, standing next to a girl in a pink blouse who was the same age as he. The girl had a dark brown complexion and long, black hair. Her arms were wrapped around his as they both smiled; although, her smile was far more genuine than his.

As Will continued to look at the photo, he began to hear a voice call out to him.

"You haven't forgotten, have you? You haven't forgotten our promise?" There was a familiar tone in the voice. To Will, it sounded like the girl in the photo, but a bit older. "You haven't forgotten our promise, have you?" The voice asked again.

Will didn't answer. Who could he possibly be talking to? The female's voice kept repeating the question, becoming louder with each repetition. Will's eyes became wider, but they were still stuck on the photo. Small beads of sweat started to run down his face. He quickly put the photo back in the notebook and tossed the notebook across the room, almost hitting the small television. He started breathing heavily, his eyes still as wide open as they were when he was looking at the photo. More sweat covered his face. Seconds later, the door to Will's room busted wide open.

"Hey!" DeMarcus said to Will. "Ma says come downstairs and eat."

Will shifted his head to the right to respond to DeMarcus. "Yeah, okay. I'll be down in a second."

DeMarcus gave Will a confused stare. He didn't ask Will if he was alright. He slowly walked away from the room, leaving the door open behind him. Will hopped up from his bed and left his room, heading for the bathroom between the stairwell and his sister's room. He turned on the sink and let the cold water run while he grabbed a hand towel from the rack above the toilet. He wiped off as much of the sweat from his face as he could; he didn't want to invoke an interrogation of any kind from his family members. With the water still running, he washed his hands with the orange-scented hand soap that was next to the sink. Finally, he shut off the water and dried his hands with the same hand towel he had wiped his head with before. Will walked down the stairs to the kitchen. Halfway down, the voice of his father bellowed from the kitchen to the staircase, "You wash your hands, boy?"

Continuing his descent down the stairs, Will answered, "Yes, sir."

In what Will could only describe as a phenomenon on the same level as the Big Bang Theory, the entire Moon family was sitting around the round glass dinner table in the middle of the kitchen, all at the same time. His mother, referred to by everyone as Liz, spent her days working as a specialist in a wellness clinic in Ingram Park's medical center after she had received her Bachelor's degree in nutrition. She was home in the afternoons, but she was normally too exhausted to cook an actual dinner. The rest of the family didn't have a problem with that, not that any of them would say that to her directly; none of them were fans of her healthy cooking.

Between July, when the family first moved to Ingram Park, and now, Will's father, Anthony had spent long hours at work as an assistant director of Information Technology at the Taylor Corporation Worldwide Headquarters downtown. The earliest he had come home on a work day was nine o'clock in the evening—the latest, two o'clock in the morning. Yet, there he was, wearing the same semi-casual apparel he was wearing when he dropped Will off from school, along with the employee badge attached to the lanyard around his neck. He was even home early enough to pick Will's seven-year-old sister, Rosetta, up from the elementary school she had started going to near the neighborhood. They were all sitting at the table, ready to eat as a family; the only thing missing was Will himself.

"Okay," Liz said to the rest of the family. "Let's say grace."

The family stood around the table, joining hands, and prayed to God to bless their meal. "Amen," they said collectively as they sat down to eat. With the exception of Liz, the members of the

Moon family inspected the contents of the plates in front of them. DeMarcus poked at the food with his fork, Rosetta tilted her head to the side to look at her plate, and Will just sat there and stared at his plate.

"Um…what is this?" Anthony asked Liz trying his best not to upset her.

Liz began to answer with a smile on her face and pride in her dish. "It's a broccoli and cheese casserole, made with low-sodium mushroom soup, light mayonnaise, egg whites, organic broccoli, and fat-free cheddar cheese." She touted the ingredients as if she were reading them from the magazine she got the recipe from. Then, as if to justify the dish's existence, she concluded with, "It's healthy."

Minutes passed, and Liz's plate was completely empty. The others' plates remained untouched. Anthony, DeMarcus, Rosetta, and Will looked at each other wondering who would be the first among them to take the first bite.

Liz noticed the four-way stare down and decided to intervene. "You don't like it, do you?" she asked the family.

Nobody would answer. Anthony still didn't want to upset her; the children stayed silent out of fear of punishment.

"I get it," Liz said calmly. "You're all still used to the way we used to eat. The constant trips to fast food restaurants, the microwave dinners, the grease pits your grandma Irene called breakfast, and Soul Food Sundays at your grandma Josephine's." Liz sprung up from her seat and walked to the refrigerator. She took a photo off of the freezer side. "But let me remind each of you what these healthier alternatives can do." She showed them the photo they must've seen about a hundred times by now.

It was of her standing in the kitchen of their previous house. For some reason, she was holding a bottle of mustard in the photo, but the main draw of the photo was the baby weight she was still carrying when the photo was taken.

Admittedly, Liz had lost a great deal of weight between then and now, and it was mostly due to her own healthy cooking. She was indeed a healthy-looking thirty-five-year-old woman. The rest of the family began eating the casserole.

Liz sat back down in her chair and crossed her arms. "So, how was the first day of school?" she asked with enthusiasm, but to none of the kids in particular.

"We gotta learn how to multiply! And we gotta learn all the states!" Rosetta blurted out.

"Yeah?" Anthony asked in response. "How many states do you know?"

Rosetta answered, "Um, let's see. There's Alabama, Alaska, Arizona…" She went on listing the names of the states in the same rhythm as the song she learned them from.

"That's great, Rosetta," Liz interrupted. "DeMarcus? How about you?"

DeMarcus answered with the utmost confidence. "Well, let's see. In first period, I got a phone number from this fine-lookin' girl. In second period, I got another one, and two more during lunch. Yeah, I'd say today was a good day."

"Uh huh," Anthony replied. "And did you learn anything important today, boy?"

DeMarcus responded, "I learned that the girls here love a brutha with an afro."

"You better not let them girls get in the way of your grades," Will's dad said. "Let them slip if you want. I've been talking to some of the people that work under me, and they told me about this all-boys military school nearby that they sent their kids to. And I'll send you, too, if you don't act right."

Meanwhile, Rosetta was still reciting the states, now to herself, "...Montana, Nebraska, Nevada..." Liz shifted her focus to Will now. This was the moment that Will feared, that he hoped would never happen but knew in his heart would.

"Well, Mr. Big High School Man. Tell us about your first day at Washington."

Will didn't look up from the plate he was slowly pecking at to answer her. "It was alright," he said quietly.

"Alright? Just alright?" She asked. "Did you find your classes okay? Do you like them? Did you join any clubs? Did you make any friends? Did you even talk to anybody?"

Will had had his fill of constant questioning for the day, so he answered each of the questions as rapidly as they were asked. "Yes ma'am. Maybe. No ma'am. Not yet. Yes, but not by choice." Will finished the casserole on his plate. He rose up from his chair and placed his plate, silverware, and cup into the empty sink.

"Where are you going? We're still talking about your day here," Liz said.

"I got homework. Don't wanna fall behind now. I don't wanna end up in some military school," Will responded, heading back upstairs.

Two hours and a few minutes passed after dinner. Will sat on his bed with an open history textbook turned to a random page beside him. He was more focused on what was being shown on the television than the text in the book, however. A knock was heard coming from his door. This was a shock to Will, considering that everyone would usually barge in when they needed him for something. Will turned the volume on the TV down with the remote in his hand. "Yes?" Will asked inviting the person knocking in.

It was his mother carrying a set of neatly folded clothes in one hand. Will noticed the clothes and asked, "Can you set them on the dresser?"

Liz responded with another question. "You're going to hang these up in your closet, right?" Will nodded, focusing back on the TV. "Yes, ma'am."

She sat the clothes on the dresser next to the other bundle of clothes from earlier. "Why didn't you put on any of the new clothes I bought you for school?" She asked sternly.

"I don't know," he answered. "Just felt comfortable in this."

"Is that the same hoodie from Salem?"

"One of them. It still fits."

Liz let out a sigh and then sat down on the bed adjacent to Will. "Look, I know these last few months haven't been easy, especially for you. A lot's happened, and most of it you really can't just get over and move on from. I know it's hard to adjust for someone like you. But we're not in the old neighborhood anymore, William. This is a new town, and you're going to a new school. This is a fresh start for you."

With his eyes still glued to the TV screen, Will rebutted, "So what? We're in a new town. That's great. That automatically means I'm supposed to forget the last few years? Like they didn't even happen?" He paused briefly and then continued, "Look, Mom. I hated Salem as much as anyone else in the family, maybe even more. And believe me when I say I'm grateful to be far away as possible from that hellhole—excuse my language. But I can't just forget what happened, like it wasn't some big deal."

Liz didn't say anything back immediately. She knew exactly what Will was referring to, but she didn't want to bring it up in conversation. "I know. But keeping to yourself isn't going to alleviate the…"

Will interrupted her. "Shh." He pointed to the TV. "Triple H is wrestling Mankind for the belt." He increased the volume on the TV, but not by much.

Liz got up from the bed and smiled. "You and your wrestling. I'll never understand it. I hear it's all scripted anyway. Well, don't stay up too late. I don't want you oversleeping and being late for school tomorrow."

"What? I gotta go back there?" Will asked with an upbeat change in his somber tone of voice. "I thought I was just visiting."

"I'm afraid you were sentenced to four years without parole," Liz answered. "Good night, Will. Make sure you brush your teeth." Liz proceeded to exit the room.

"Yes, ma'am. Good night."

***

A breeze wafted through the air. Patches of green grass covered the ground, and a clear blue sky consumed the horizon. There were a few clouds, but not enough to cover the bright sun. In the distance, there was a set of swings from a playground. One of the swings was empty, but the other was occupied by a child. The child seemed to be about eight or nine years old and bore a resemblance to William. His hands gripped the chains that suspended the seat, and he looked down at the ground, kicking each of his legs simultaneously. They couldn't be seen, but there were other children playing around the younger-looking Will, whose voices could be heard.

"Why do you hang out with him? He's weird."

"Yeah, he never says anything."

"Plus, he sucks at basketball."

"All he does is read those books. What a scrub."

"Hey, wait! Where you going? Man, she's as hopeless as he is. C'mon, y'all, let's go somewhere else."

The voices faded away, and a shadowy figure approached the swing set. It wasn't clear who the figure was at first, but as it drew nearer, it began to resemble a young girl, about the same age as the young Will. She sat on the empty swing next to him and smiled at him. The blue sky became white. Then the green grass became white. White consumed everything, including the two children and the swing set.

There was no sound, save for a constant flat beep in a familiar pitch and tone that steadily increased in volume. It was faint, but between the beeps another familiar voice called out, "You haven't forgotten, have you? You haven't forgotten our promise?"

"URGH!" Will screamed out. His head sprang from the pillows on his bed. Breathing heavily, he extended his hands toward the front of him to see the sweat on his palms. He hopped out of the bed and reached for the light switch on the wall next to the door. With a better sense of vision, Will walked to the dresser and stood in front of it, staring at his reflection at the mirror placed on top of it. After taking a few more short breaths, he looked behind him to the part of the floor near the TV where the notebook from earlier still sat. Will noticed that the photo was barely sticking out of the notebook.

Strangely enough, Will didn't return the notebook to the dresser from where he got it from. Instead, he placed it in his backpack. For the remainder of the evening, he laid across his bed with his eyes wide open.

Chapter Five

The morning sky was clear, but the sun hadn't completely risen yet. There was still a bit of a summer breeze in the air, but it was faint. In a few days, it would be replaced by the winds of autumn. Will pulled his portable CD player from out of the pockets of the same hoodie he was wearing yesterday. He turned it to track eleven, put on his earbuds, and pressed the play button. Gang Starr's "You Know My Steez" played at a low volume from the earbuds as he walked down the street on his way to school. He approached the intersection where the bus dropped off the other kids from school yesterday and saw a group of them standing by waiting for it. He was walking by the other kids, not paying much attention to them, when someone in the group shouted out to him.

"DUDE!" Nathan called out. Will turned his head to the side and pulled out one of his earbuds. Holding a skateboard, Nathan ran from out of the group of kids waiting at the bus stop to catch up with Will.

"Um…Nathan right?" Will asked.

"Yeah dude! I thought I saw you walking home yesterday," Nathan replied. "You always walk to and from school?"

"Yeah, I guess."

Will started walking again with one earbud still in his ear, and Nathan started walking beside him. Will was surprised, but he didn't show it. He also didn't do anything to dismiss Nathan either. "That's cool, dude. I'll walk with ya. I don't need the bus driver giving me crap about my board again. Plus, ya know, there aren't any chicks on there."

Will asked, "Chicks? I saw some girls at that stop."

"Yeah, but none of them are my type." Nathan rebutted. "I like the ones with a lot to offer in the chest region, if you know what I mean."

Will didn't answer. He just kept walking with his hands in hoodie pockets.

"Yeah, you know what I mean," Nathan continued with a chuckle and a devious grin on his face.

The boys kept walking to school on the same route Will had used the day before. There was a bit of an awkward silence for a while.

"I take it you're not much of a talker, dude," Nathan said to Will.

"Not really," Will answered; he kept looking forward rather than at Nathan to reply.

"Eh, it's cool, dude, probably just nervousness getting to ya. You're kinda new here, right? Still probably just getting used to the place, so I get it."

Will shifted his focus on Nathan now. "Yeah, that's it."

Nathan responded. "Tell ya what. Stick with me, dude. I'll show ya the ropes. I've lived in this neighborhood pretty much all my life, and I know this place like the back of my hand. More importantly, I'll show ya where the really *really* hot chicks hang out!" At that moment, a melody chimed from Nathan's left pocket. "Hold your excitement for a second, dude. I gotta take this." Nathan reached into his pocket and pulled out his cell phone.

He answered, "What's up, Ash? Nah, I'm walking with my new friend… Yeah, from the cafeteria… Relax, I'm pretty sure he's legit… No, I don't think he's with the government… Yeah, I'll get you one from the store. Blueberry, right? Okay, cool. See ya in a few." Nathan hung up the phone, put it back into his pocket, and said to Will, "We gotta make a quick pit stop, dude."

The two made their way to the convenience store on the corner of Benbrook and Chisholm. Nathan opened the entrance door, and as they entered the store, they were greeted with an electronic chime heard throughout the store. Also heard throughout the store was the shout of the clerk working the register in the front, "BACKPACKS!" The clerk pointed to an area near the door where Will and Nathan were standing; a sign that was taped on the wall above the area read, "Students must place their backpacks here when entering."

Nathan and Will placed their backpacks, along with Nathan's skateboard, in the designated area and proceeded to the back of the store.

"Oh, thank God," Nathan proclaimed as he grabbed the very last individually-wrapped blueberry muffin from the rack.

They didn't go back to the register area immediately. Nathan browsed nearly every other aisle, adding with the muffin two different bags of potato chips, a small box of cookies, a beef jerky stick, and a twenty-ounce bottle of Pepsi from the freezer. "Ah! Breakfast of champions!" Nathan exclaimed.

Will and Nathan approached the cashier. Nathan placed the snacks on the counter, and the cashier began to ring them up. Will noticed that with each item that the cashier ran through the scanner, he gave Nathan more and more of a disgruntled look.

This clerk wasn't like any other convenience store cashiers Will had ever come across. For one, he was a Caucasian man. He was much older, too. It was as if he'd lived a life full of experiences, both good and bad. Something must've happened to have driven the man to convince himself that he should spend his remaining years working at a convenience store. The clerk definitely gave Will the impression that he both resented and envied the young, especially those who frequented the store, and truly believed that youth was wasted on them. But the biggest contrasts Will noticed between this particular clerk and those he had shopped with in the past were that this clerk wasn't behind a thick layer of bullet-proof glass, he wasn't talking to Nathan through an intercom, and Nathan didn't have to hand him the money owed via a pull-out tray.

The clerk handed Nathan his change and two plastic bags. One contained just the blueberry muffin, and the other contained all of the other items he purchased. He put the latter of the two bags in his backpack and held on to the bag with the muffin, being extra careful with it. With their belongings back in their possession, the two boys exited the store.

Right as they stepped outside, they were greeted by a group of kids. It was the same group that Will had seen loitering outside the store yesterday. Now that Will could get a closer look at the group, the resemblance to Nathan as far as clothing and appearance was closer than Will had previously theorized. However, this time Will wasn't taken aback by their looks, but rather their smell. Coming off of them was an odor very similar to the smells that came off of people from the areas of Salem that Will's parents told him and his brother to stay far away from.

"'Sup, Nate?" One of the boys in the group asked in a monotone voice.

"Nothin' much, dude. Just heading to school," Nathan answered.

"School? That's so lame. Ditch that crap, and hang with us today," said the one girl in the group.

"Yeah, man. We're hitting up that abandoned strip mall on Bartley. My man Craig's hooking us up with some primo stuff, too. Gonna blaze all day," said another boy.

"Sounds like fun, dudes," Nathan responded. "But you know Ashley. She'll kill me if I don't get this muffin to her. Plus, I gotta show the newbie here the ropes. Don't want him to get eaten by the sharks on the second day, ya know?"

"Pfft, whatever. Learn some geo-alge-trigo-history whatever for us," another boy said. The group let out small, muffled laughs.

Nathan and Will continued their walk to school—they were minutes away from the campus now. Even with the stop at the convenience store, the walk to school today seemed much shorter in time than the walk home yesterday. Maybe it was because Will wasn't walking alone, and making conversation had a way of killing the time. "You hang out with those guys?" Will asked Nathan.

"Yeah, we all skate together sometimes," Nathan answered.

"Hmmm," Will said.

"Oh dude, don't worry. I don't smoke pot like them," Nathan said under the impression that that was where the conversation was going.

"Doesn't bother me," Will said. "That stuff is everywhere. Probably the first and only thing Ingram Park has in common with my old town."

Nathan let out a chuckle. "Wish my old man was as chill about it as you are, dude. He'd ship me off to that boys-only military school if he caught me with that stuff! Besides, those guys' peer pressure won't work on me. I've known them for years; they aren't really in a position to call anyone lame for not wanting to ditch school and get high."

"They aren't?" Will asked.

"No way, dude. Back in junior high, they were all on the Honor Society, and I don't think there was a single missed day of school between the four of them."

"You're kidding." Will said.

"Nope. And consider that lesson one of suburban life, dude. There's much more to people than how they look and how they act. And on that note, I gotta deliver this muffin before homeroom."

Before he knew it, Will was standing on the quad area of Washington's campus near the statue he saw yesterday. He saw Nathan walk off in the distance. He placed the other earbud in his ear and proceeded to the E building where his locker and homeroom class were. It was much easier to find the building now. Will found his locker down the hall from his homeroom class.

"Let's see...35...19...21," Will read the combination of his locker from another crinkled piece of paper different from the one with his class schedule. Will started inputting the combination to his locker. It wasn't any different from the locker in his middle school. With ease, Will opened his locker and just started throwing all of the textbooks from his backpack to the locker in an unorganized fashion. Before Will could close his locker door, he heard a loud slam nearby.

"Damn, son! What y'all trippin' for?!" It was Rob from Will's homeroom class. He was slammed against the locker next to Will's. He was being accosted by three large, menacing-looking boys. One of the boys grabbed Rob and asked, "Where's our money, you little fraud?!"

"Yo! I told y'all, you get when I got it! But how I'm supposed to be on my hustle and get my money up when I gotta deal wit' y'all all the time?"

"Screw this. I say we just beat him down and be done with it," one of the other boys said, cracking his knuckles.

"C'mon, y'all, we ain't gotta resort to violence. Erase the hate. Increase the peace," Rob said hesitantly. He started sweating.

Will closed his locker door. He tried to walk away as this wasn't his fight. But Rob looked to his right and noticed Will. "Will, homie! Tell me you ain't just gonna sit there and let these clowns mob up on your boy like this!"

Will didn't know how to respond. He wasn't officially friends with Rob. He didn't owe him anything and had no obligation to help him.

The third boy of the group asked, "Oh, so you're with him? Maybe we should mess you up, too!"

Rob's demeanor went from fearful to cocky in an instant. He touted, "Say, fool, you don't wanna mess with my mans over here. This homie right here from Salem. Yeah, THAT Salem, the one that's always on *Cops*, son. And let me tell you about my homie over here. He ain't need to roll deep! He rolled through the toughest hoods by himself and put everybody that stepped to him in check. So, I don't know 'bout y'all, but I'm sayin' if it was me, if it was me tho', I wouldn't get on his bad side, son!"

Will looked at the boys with the same nonchalant look he had been giving pretty much everyone so far. Just then, the three boys ran off quickly.

"YEAH, YOU FOOLS BETTER GET GHOST! AND DON'T EVER TRY TO RUN UP ON BIG ROB DAWG AGAIN!" Rob shouted while grabbing his crotch area, for some reason. Then, as best as he could, he let out a few barking sounds imitating some of the fiercest dogs known. Once again, Will didn't say anything. He just gave Rob the same blank stare he had in class yesterday. At that moment, a large hand gripped one of Will's shoulders and one of Rob's. The two turned around to see a towering figure standing behind them. "What's up, Mr. Terrell?" Rob asked nervously.

***

The homeroom bell rang, and chimes sounded from the intercom.

"Good morning, students, faculty, and staff of Washington High School. This is Principal Caine speaking. I just want to remind you that the dogs accompanying the security officers are here to do a job. Please refrain from interrupting them by petting them and adoring how cute they are. No, you may not take them home with you. And no, you may not give them cute pet names like 'Bubbles' or 'Snowflake.' Also, students, please remember to bus your lunch trays when you're done eating. Don't leave them on the tables for the cafeteria staff to retrieve. Washington can ill afford another lunch lady strike, nor can it afford any medical expenses as a result of said strike. With that said, let's have both a fun and fulfilling day full of educational experiences!"

Once again, Will was late for homeroom class. Only this time, he wasn't roaming the halls looking for his class. He was sitting in a chair in the administration office. Across from Will was the secretary, a middle-aged woman frantically pressing the keys on her computer's keyboard, breaking away only to answer the constantly ringing phone on her desk with, "Washington High. Please hold." Will couldn't get a good glimpse of the woman; her desk was flooded with stacks of papers and folders covering nearly all of her body. A door to the left of Will with a sign reading "Vice-Principal" opened.

It was Rob who walked out the door. "Yeah whatever, busta," Rob mumbled so softly that only he could hear it. He walked towards Will, putting on a belt that he didn't have before and that clearly didn't fit him.   "This right here is some booty," Rob complained. "I got two more days of detention on top of what I got yesterday, AND I gotta wear this lame belt. Terrell got me out here looking like a straight-up scrub! How I'm supposed to mack on the shorties, when I got my pants higher up than Urkel, son?"

For the first time, Will responded to Rob's forced urban dialect. "I guess you'll have to put your pimpin' on hold for a day."

"Nah, homie," Rob replied. "The pimp game don't never stop for nothin'. Ayo, good lookin' out havin' my back like that earlier. I knew you had that thug mentality in you."

"What happened to 'I do my own dirt, put in my own work?'" Will asked referring to Rob's previous boasts.

"Shoot man, I was just testing you. Seeing if you was legit, or if you was just some geek off the streets pretending to be hood. Appearances ain't everything around here, homie. Remember that." Rob left the administration office.

Even if Will had had the words to rebut Rob's ironic statement, he was far too dumbstruck at the fact that Rob would even say something like that to even form them. From the vice-principal's office, a shout of "MOON!" was bellowed.

Will entered the office of Vice-Principal Maurice Terrell and sat in one of the two wooden chairs across from his desk. Terrell's face was covered, at first, by a folder with Will's full name on it. Large, dark black, muscular hands gripped each end of the folder as Terrell continued to read to himself. During the time of silence, Will took a look around the office and noticed the several trophies, award plaques, and other various accolades awarded to Vice-Principal Terrell for his tenure as both a football player and coach. On a shelf to the left sat frames containing pictures of Terrell shaking hands with prominent football players and coaches from both the college level and the professional league. The walls were plastered with plaques framing clipped newspaper articles and magazine covers featuring Terrell and his accomplishments on the field. The largest plaque was placed right above Terrell himself. Framed inside was a copy of his Bachelor's in Education degree from Tuskegee University.

Vice-Principal Terrell placed the folder down on his desk. He was wearing thin, square-rimmed glasses coated in sterling silver. He had a bit more hair than Will. It was black for the most part, but touches of gray looked like they were starting to come in. He also had a full set of sideburns that ran into his short beard and goatee. He was dressed in a grey, sleeveless argyle sweater vest; underneath was a white long-sleeved dress shirt that did a poor job of hiding his muscles, along with a grey-and-black-striped tie.

"I've been looking over your record, Moon," Vice-Principal Terrell said. "In your middle school, you maintained a C average. You spent a couple days in both In-School and

Out-of-School Suspension for fighting and other offences, and you didn't belong to any extracurricular clubs or activities." Terrell paused for a moment and continued, "You have all the makings of a problem child, something I've seen many, many times before. And the fact that you're in my office, on, what, the second day? That all but confirms it.

"Now, I could give you a few days of detention like I did your friend, Mr. Stanley. But then, you'd be just another disciplinary statistic. We'd be doing this all year, back and forth, until Principal Caine or I had enough and just expelled you, or worse. But I look at you, and I don't see a problem child. I see a misguided soul with no direction who just happened to fall in with the wrong crowd. And I wouldn't be doing my job as an educator if I didn't put you on the right path."

Terrell turned to the computer on his desk and started typing. "So, in lieu of detention, Mr. Moon, I am signing you up for the Washington High Booster Club. You'll help organize school events and set up for them and break them down when they're done."

Will's eyes sprung open in shock at the news. Terrell was right; he hadn't been a part of any club or activity in the past, and he certainly had no intention of doing otherwise.

"According to their page on the school's website, I believe they're still setting up for Friday's game. So, after school you will report to them at the athletics complex down the street. I trust you know what building I'm talking about."

Will answered softly, "Yes, sir."

Terrell shifted away from the computer and pulled out a slip from one of the drawers on his desk. He pulled a black pen from the football helmet-shaped pen holder and started writing on the slip. "Good. This way, you'll surround yourself with positive members of your peer group. In turn, you'll feel good about yourself and want to do well. Now, take this pass and go straight to your class." He extended his hand to give the slip to Will. Will got out of the chair and took the pass from Terrell. Just as he was leaving the office, Terrell stopped him. "You were lost before. I see that. But this will put you back on the path, Mr. Moon." Saying nothing in return, Will exited the office.

Chapter Six

The bell for lunch period rang. Will waited in the back of the classroom until his classmates were done scrambling with one another in a desperate attempt to leave the class as soon as possible. With earbuds firmly placed in his ears and hands in his hoodie pockets, Will made his way to the cafeteria. With the music playing in his ears, Will tried to block out the noise around him. He wanted just a few minutes to himself for the first time today, but since he knew that wasn't going to get it, this would have to do.

Will arrived at the quad area. This time, it was completely occupied by students. There were small tables made of stone that were filled by random students, some of which included: a group of gossiping girls, more kids bearing Nathan's resemblance, some kids with their noses buried in books, and a group of kids dressed in all black sitting at a table almost completely canopied by the shadows of a large tree.

A lot of students formed lines behind each other at the four payphones near a staircase, waiting for their turns to use one of the phones. It reminded Will of a scene from a prison movie; he wondered if one of the students was going to blurt out, "Phone check, fool." Finally, a group of girls stood by the stone fountain in the middle of the quad in adoration of a boy strumming a guitar who paid no attention to them. The noise outside was far louder than it had been in the cafeteria yesterday. Will couldn't hear a single sound from his earbuds, not even with the CD player set to maximum volume. So, he turned it off, placed the earbuds back in his pockets, and bobbed and weaved his way through the crowd to the cafeteria.

As soon as he entered the cafeteria, Will saw Nathan sitting at the table the two had eaten at yesterday, but there wasn't a lunch tray near Nathan. Nathan spotted Will entering the cafeteria, grabbed his backpack, and launched out of his chair to meet him halfway between the table and the entrance.

"Let's go, dude," Nathan said to Will. He turned Will around and playfully shoved him back outside.

"Go? Go where?" Will asked, still being shoved.

Back outside, Nathan answered, "To the library. Time you met Ashley."

"But I'm hungry," Will moaned. His stomach rumbled a little bit.

Nathan reached into his backpack and pulled out a bag of potato chips from the convenience store. "Here, dude," he said handing the bag to Will. "You don't wanna be eating too much of that cafeteria slop. It'll kill you." Nathan continued with a haunting emphasis, "Literally...kill you."

Will took the bag, opened it, and started eating the chips. "Thanks. But why are we meeting Ashley now?" he asked while still eating.

Nathan answered, "I told her about you, and she said she wanted to meet you ASAP." Nathan continued with a smirk on his face, "Maybe she's got a crush on you."

Will let out a small gasp. Then Nathan said with a devious tone, "Or maybe she wants to pick your brain for some experiment."

Will's second gasp was more loud and noticeable. He even dropped the potato chip he had in his hand at the time.

Nathan shrugged his shoulders and nonchalantly concluded, "Eh, you can't be too sure with her. C'mon, dude!"

The two walked to the library. It was in the B building that was in the exact middle of the campus. All of the classroom buildings were connected to this one via outdoor walkways. At two stories high, the library itself dominated the majority of the B building. The top floor was covered corner to corner by towering shelves filled with books. There were bookshelves on the bottom floor, as well, but for the most part there were circular tables and the librarians' counter. One of the tables was rectangular. There were eight wooden separators on this table. Between each of the separators were desktop computers that looked to be about two years old. There was complete silence in the library. Not too many students were there, save for a couple making out between two of the bookshelves and a girl sitting at one of the computers.

Nathan pointed at the girl at the computer and quietly said to Will, "There she is, dude."

Nathan and Will approached Ashley, and Nathan tapped on her shoulder. "Well it's about time," Ashley said, still looking at the screen. She pulled her chair from out under the table and got up from it. She turned around to greet the boys. Ashley looked exactly as Nathan had described her to Will; however, he had failed to mention her braces. Her wardrobe was more conservative in comparison with other girls Will had seen around campus. She was wearing a yellow-and-white-striped polo and navy blue medium wash jeans.

Ashley extended her hand out to the boys, but it wasn't for a handshake. "Muffin?" she demanded.

Nathan reached into his backpack, pulled out a muffin wrapped in several napkins, and handed it to Ashley. She unwrapped the muffin and started furiously eating it without hesitation or pause. She tore into the muffin as if she were a lioness in the wild digging into her prey, yet not a single crumb dropped to the ground.

"This is Will, by the way," Nathan said sarcastically. Just as fast as she had started eating the muffin, Ashley finished it. She wiped her hands with the napkins that had previously wrapped the muffin.

"It's nice to meet you, Will," Ashley said.

"Um...likewise," Will responded nervously.

"Well, looks like you two are off to a great start," Nathan intervened. "I'll leave y'all to it. I saw this pretty cute girl over in the fiction section. What? You two ain't the only ones that get to make new friends!" Nathan walked off.

Ashley grabbed her red backpack from under the chair she was previously sitting in. She started walking towards one of the unoccupied circular tables in the middle of the library. "Nathan tells me you're from Salem," she said to Will. Will followed her to the table, and the two took seats across from each other.

"Yeah," Will responded.

"I've only heard stories about that place; I've read articles online and in magazines. I heard it's been going downhill since after the civil rights movement of the sixties."

"I wouldn't know about all that. But yeah, life in Salem wasn't pretty."

"And yet, here you are, as alive as the day you were born. That's gotta count for something right?"

"I guess."

Ashley crossed her arms and leaned in a little towards Will. "So tell me, how are you enjoying suburban life so far?" she asked.

Will reluctantly answered, "It's...uh...quiet."

"Yeah, I suppose it is. But quiet is boring, wouldn't you agree?" Ashley asked. She continued, "You've been here for a few months, right? In that time, haven't you asked yourself, 'Is this all there is?' just once?"

Will didn't answer. Of course he had never asked himself that question, but he couldn't bring himself to say so.

Ashley unfolded her arms and interlocked her fingers. "Will, you now go to school with the sons and daughters of holders of high positions within the Taylor Corporation, one the biggest multinational conglomerates of the world, if not the biggest."

Will responded, "And?"

Ashley continued, "Most of us were born here. Out-of-towners like yourself are a rare commodity. We live a life of moderate privilege, never wanting or needing anything for long. At the price of working insanely long hours right under the man himself, our parents fulfill our every desire without the need for us to break a single sweat ourselves. And as a result, we get bored."

Ashley paused for a moment. She knew this was a lot for Will to take in. But she pressed on, "That boredom drives us to do things we probably shouldn't. Some of us resort to recreational drugs and other vices. Others perform misdemeanors, hoping to not get caught, but they brag about them to their peers for temporary accolade, regardless. Some of us seek to ruin the lives others, if only to fill the void in our own. Some of us break the hearts of many to compensate for the love we don't feel from our parents. And some of us craft brand new personas for ourselves, with zero regard for peer approval. Just to give a few examples."

Will asked, "Why are you telling me all of this?"

Ashley replied, "Because when I first looked into your half-opened eyes, I could tell that you're bored. You haven't even been here for a year. And yet you've got that same bored look that everyone else gets. So I'm curious, what will you do to alleviate that boredom?"

Will became a bit defensive with Ashley at this point. "So what?" he asked. "I like it boring. I like being able to walk down my street without having to worry about getting jumped because I have textbooks in my hand. I like the sleep I get from not hearing police sirens blaring all night. And I like knowing my parents are gonna come home every night safe and sound. Just to give a few examples." He spoke the last part in a sarcastic tone, mimicking Ashley.

Will got up from his chair and grabbed his backpack. "I don't know what you were expecting from this little meeting, but, by all means, do whatever you feel you need to do to relieve your boredom. Just keep me out of it," he said to Ashley.

Will stormed to the library's exit while Ashley remained at the table by herself for a few minutes. Nathan eventually joined her, sporting a bright red handprint across his right cheek.

Ashley noticed the slap mark and smiled as she asked Nathan, "Laid it on a bit too thick?"

"I was about to ask you the same question," Nathan responded with a matching smirk.

"Perhaps," Ashley answered. "But I got all the information I need about him. His few words leave me to believe that he's lived a troubling life, to say the least. I expected that much when I pulled up his record and learned where he was from. Because of that, he's formed a nearly impenetrable shell around himself. It's going to be a while before he truly adjusts to life here, and it's not going to be easy for him. But I'm still confident we can help him, and he, in turn, can help us. Thanks for bringing him to me."

There was still some time left in lunch period, but Will didn't go back to the cafeteria. Instead, he headed to his locker to get his textbook for the next class. His hands remained in his pockets the entire trek, but Will didn't put back on his earbuds. The E building was entirely empty at the time. The silence would've been haunting for most, but for Will it was serene.

Will still had a sour look on his face as he opened his locker. What Ashley said to him in the library weighed heavily on his mind, and it hurt his head thinking about it. There was clearly a difference in the life he had once lived and the one he was living now. The things Ashley was talking about… Will wasn't unfamiliar with them. His peers in Salem did things like that all the time. But they did them because they claimed they needed to survive or wanted to get rich. Or they just wanted to forget about life and all its shortcomings in general. So Will was having a hard time believing that anyone would want to do things like that just out of sheer boredom.

But then, he thought about people like Rob, and those kids from the convenience store—how Nathan said those kids were completely different a year ago, and how Rob was pretending to be something he clearly wasn't. Will's head was still in his locker. He was just standing there thinking about these things. But he had had enough thinking. He slowly closed his locker when he noticed a girl casually standing against the locker near his.

"So you have forgotten," the girl said to Will. She bore a resemblance all too familiar to Will—the one of the girl in the photo—but she looked and sounded a few months older than that girl. Her hair was relaxed and hung down past her shoulders. She was wearing an all-white dress, similar to those Will had seen worn by the ladies at his old church, along with a matching pair of high heels.

Will wasn't sure if the girl was real or a figment of his imagination. Regardless, he asked, "Forgotten what?"

"You did forget!" the girl answered with a disappointed look. "You forgot the promise we made! Don't pinky swears mean anything to you?"

Will was taken aback. This was the girl from the photo and from the dream he had last night! But she was a bit older. "This can't be right," Will said in disbelief.

"So, did you forget our promise or not?" she asked again. The girl waited for a response, but Will wouldn't give one.

Persistently, she added, "Well?! Did you, Will?!"

"I DIDN'T FORGET!" Will shouted as he slammed one of his fists against his locker. But he was only shouting to himself now. The girl was gone, vanished without a trace as if she were never there to begin with. The bell for the next period rang. Slowly, the building became flooded with students again.

Chapter Seven

Will stood in front of a white canvas placed on a wooden easel in a circle composed of the other students of his first-level art class and their easels. In the middle of the circle was the teacher, Ms. Johansen. She looked to be in her late twenties to early thirties. She had long, flowing, curly, auburn hair. She wore purple thick-rimmed glasses, which complimented the plain purple T-shirt that was covered by a paint-stained navy blue apron.

Ms. Johansen gave a passionate address to the class in a soothing voice. "Now, students. I will not tell you what to paint as I am but an observer. Who am I to dictate what the creator creates? But as you begin your painting, remember that you are not just applying paint to the canvas. With every stroke, you are pouring your emotions, your essence, your very being onto that canvas. When your work is complete, we will not see just a painting, but also the very contents of your soul! Paint on, my students! Show me your souls!" Her body language gave off the same impassioned feel as her speech.

The students began painting. While some struggled, others seemed to have no problem painting. It was as if they'd painted a million times before and no longer needed any instruction; this class was nothing more than a necessary elective and an easy "A." Will, on the other hand, was on neither side of that coin. His canvas remained as untouched as it had been at the beginning of the class. He had a brush in his hand, and there was paint on it, but as time passed, the paint had completely dried.

Ms. Johansen began walking around the class with her hands clasped behind her back. She observed the students' works and gave brief criticisms to each of them. "Excellent work, Aubrey. Pay attention to your strokes, Brandon. More saturation in that tree, Stephanie. It's coming along nicely, Michael." Ms. Johansen finally came to a student who had her hand up and had been trying to grab her attention for at least five minutes. "Yes, what is it, Brittany?" she asked.

The girl answered, "I'm out of red paint. Do we have any more?"

"I am afraid not," Ms. Johansen said. Her tone of her voice went from that of devotion to despair. "This is why I emailed your parents that list of needed supplies. Budget cutbacks mean you will need to bring in some of your own supplies to complete your art. Until then, you'll have to make do with the paints we do have available." She became excited once again. She smiled and said, "But you know, there's no rule or law that says cherries have to be red."

Brittany continued painting, now with more enthusiasm than before.

Ms. Johansen eventually came around to Will and noticed the blank canvas. "Is there a problem, William?" she asked him.

"I have no idea what to paint," Will said.

"I see. Tell me, William, at this very moment, what is on your mind?"

Will rolled his eyes as he answered, "A whole bunch of stuff, none of which makes any sense. How can I put it in a way you'd understand? Right now, my mind is like one of those five-hundred-piece puzzles. The pieces are scattered all over the floor, and a lot of them are missing from the box."

"How very profound," Johansen said. "And yet, is there anything within that chaos that stands out? A beacon of light among the darkness? A silver lining in your cloud of thoughts?"

Without answering, Will sighed and bent down to open his backpack. He pulled out the old notebook from his dresser and pulled out the photo from last night. He grabbed a thumbtack from the table behind him and affixed the photo to the top left corner of the canvas. "I'll leave you to it then," Ms. Johansen said with a look of satisfaction as she walked to the next student.

It wasn't Will's intention to recreate the photo. He only sought to use it as a reference. In reality, he wanted to paint a picture of the girl who he thought he had seen in the hallway about an hour ago, the one who spoke to him. "I didn't forget," Will whispered softly to himself. He applied a fresh coat of paint to his brush and started adding strokes to the canvas.

Two hours and another class period later, the final bell for the day rang. Will headed towards the bus stop and parking lot area as he had done the day before. He wanted to go home as soon as possible, but he remembered that he had other obligations. From the lot, Will looked westward. In the distance, he spotted the massive structure which was to be his next destination. Vice-Principal Terrell was right; Will couldn't miss that thing even if he tried to.

Will began walking on the sidewalk towards the building. Between it and the campus were large fields of green grass that blew in the gentle wind that filled the air. In the middle of the field was a wonder Will have had never seen before in his life, one he had never thought conceivable. It was a Taco King restaurant, a Pizza Lord restaurant, and a Baron's Chicken restaurant, all in the same building! As he walked past the restaurant combo, he gazed at it in amazement, with his eyes and his jaw wide open. Behind the miracle of science that was the restaurant combo, there was a huge movie theater. The sign in the parking touted that the theater had eighteen screens and was currently showing movies Will have had no interest in watching. Ultimately, between the mall a few minutes' walk away from the school, the restaurants, and the movie theater, there were many places students of Washington High could go if they chose to ditch class.

It took about five minutes for Will to reach his destination, the Northside School District Athletic Complex. He had to walk through the massive parking lot. It took him almost three times as long for him to do so as it had taken for him to get there.

But when he did, he got a close-up look at the building. Upon closer inspection, it was easy to compare its size to the famous colosseum of ancient Rome. The last and only time Will had seen anything remotely similar to its stature was about two years ago, when his dad drove him and his brother quite a distance out of town to see Chris Benoit against Meng in a death match and Dean Malenko wrestling Jeff Jarrett for the heavyweight title.

The most interesting thing about the enormous structure, however, was the sign planted into the ground near the entrance. Will glanced at the sign for a moment and learned that the stadium had been recently renovated. According to the sign, the project, which took eighteen months to complete, was a major overhaul with a sixty-three-million-dollar price tag. Some of this sum was donated by the Taylor Corporation along with smaller local businesses, but most of it was provided by the taxpayers. "That could've bought a whole lot of red paint," Will commented to himself.

Will walked through the interior of the stadium and, in time, found himself standing near the fifty-yard line of the football field. There were other students on the field, frantically running around performing various tasks. There were also a few students in several locations in the stands setting up banners and such. On the right thirty-yard line was a tall, skinny male shouting commands through a megaphone. "Get those fireworks counted! I don't want a single one missing! You better make sure those words programmed into the display board are spelled right! YOU! YEAH, YOU! DON'T FOCUS ON ME! PAY ATTENTION WITH THAT BANNER! DO NOT TEAR IT!

May God have mercy on you if you do, because I will not!" It was safe to say this was the guy Will was to report to.

Will approached the boy, who was still screaming commands at the top of his lungs through the megaphone. His voice was flamboyant, a trait given away by his overall posture and the white frosted tips of his spiky hair.

"Uh…excuse me," Will uttered to him.

"YES?!" The boy said to Will still through the megaphone. Will covered his ears, writhing in a sharp pain from being that close to the megaphone and its feedback. "Oh, apologies," the boy said after he lowered the megaphone from his mouth. "Yes?"

After his ears stopped ringing, Will continued to speak with him. "My name is William Moon. Is this the booster club?"

"Why, yes, it is. Terrell said you'd be coming. You must be his 'pet project' for this semester. Look, William Moon, I don't need you here, and you certainly don't look like you want to be here. So why don't you just walk around and make sure there isn't any trash on the ground. Do a good job and I'll tell Terrell you were a good little boy who participated, m'kay?"

Despite obviously being talked down to, Will didn't object to the young man's request. "Okay," Will agreed semi-optimistically.

"Good," the boy said as he handed Will a large roll of black trash bags.

Will walked away to begin his task while another walked up to him.

"Drew, we've got four hundred fireworks, way more than we need," the girl said.

"Oh, you poor, deluded child," Drew responded patting the girl on her head in a condescending manner. "There's no such thing as 'way more than we need.' If those rubes in the student council didn't screw me on the budget, we'd have way more. Now, get the displays set up and double check to make sure none of those fireworks are duds. Come Friday night, this sky is gonna light up like the freakin' sun, and those plebeians in the cheap seats are going to love me for it." The girl started to walk off when Drew used the megaphone to conclude, "And do NOT deviate from my blueprints! Remember, you are only here to make my visions a reality."

There wasn't much trash for Will to pick up. Even the stands were nearly litter-free. Still, Will leisurely strolled the field looking for some to pick up. He didn't want to tell Drew he was done. In fact, he wanted neither another conversation with him, nor another assigned task.

No other member of the booster club approached Will. They didn't wonder who he was or why he was walking around looking for trash that wasn't there. It wasn't from lack of interest, however. Every member was far too focused with obeying the never-ending stream of commands being blurted from Drew's megaphone. Drew's voice through his megaphone only got louder with every command as time went on. It even drowned out the music being played through Will's earbuds.

Some time passed as a gradient of royal blue and orange filled the sky. Now, standing next to Krystal, the girl from the statue, Drew gave one more command from his megaphone. "Okay people wrap it up! We're done for the day! You've all done a great job. And by 'you,' I mean me!"

The other members of the booster club concluded their tasks and began leaving the field through the many corridors in the stadium. Will tied up the only trash bag he had filled using its drawstrings and deposited it into one of the large garbage bins nearby. He grabbed his backpack from the stands and headed to the nearest corridor to the parking lot.

In the dimly lit corridor, Will found himself walking, with his hands in his pockets, behind two boys. He wasn't sure if the two knew he was a few paces behind them. Regardless, they had a conversation Will couldn't help overhearing.

"You hear anything else about F2?"

"Word is, they're gonna announce if it's going down tomorrow night."

"Oh man, I hope it is. I've already got a spot picked."

"Yeah, but shut up. You know we're not supposed to talk about it out loud."

"Dude, it's just us here."

"Yeah, but still…"

The conversation ended there and Will didn't think too much about it. He exited the stadium and found himself back out in the parking lot. He kept walking for a while, but eventually he stopped long enough to put his earbuds back in, resuming his music. Will had successfully put in the right earbud, but as he was about to put on the left, a blue, four-door car pulled up right by him. Will was a bit spooked. He wondered if those two boys did know he was behind him. Did Will overhear something he wasn't supposed to? Just then, the window to the passenger side of the car rolled down; it was Krystal.

She popped her head out from the window and asked Will, "Need a ride?"

Will was skeptical about riding in a car with people he barely knew. But on that same note, he had had more than his fill of physical exertion for the day. Will entered the backseat door on Krystal's side of the car and placed his backpack next to him. The inside was a bit cramped for Will. Krystal had her seat back further than the driver, and his football equipment took up the other backseat. Will didn't want to inconvenience Krystal, so at no time during the ride did he ask her to move her seat up. "Thanks," he said to the two in the front, as the driver put the car back in motion.

"You're welcome," Krystal responded. "Oh, by the way. This is Eddie, my boyfriend."

"Uh…hi, Eddie," Will greeted nervously.

"What's going on, man? I'd shake your hand but you know, ten and two," Eddie replied with his eyes still focused on the road ahead of him. "Where are we headed?" he asked.

"Um…Presley Place," Will answered.

"Oh cool, same neighborhood as us. Never seen you around before, though. You from out of town?"

"Yeah, moved here in July," Will said.

"Where from?"

"Northeast," Will said. He could've said Salem, but so far, giving that answer had started conversations that he hadn't been too fond of, and he certainly didn't want another to start another one.

Krystal chimed in to change the conversation. "So, Will, how are you enjoying high school so far?"

Will said, "Let's just say I hate it when TV lies to me." He was referring to the numerous television sitcoms he had watched that took place in a high school, where even the most trying conflicts could be solved within thirty minutes and the quarrelling cast members forgave each other's transgressions, learned something the show deemed important, and ended the show with a hearty laugh amongst them as they consumed whatever corporate product was sponsoring the show that week.

The two in the front let out a loud, uncontrollable laugh in response to Will's answer. Krystal said to Will, "Don't sweat it. You'll get used to everything, and this will be a breeze for you. Of course, it's easier when you've got friends with you. Have you made any yet?"

"Kinda," Will said.

"Well, that's a good start. Also, don't be afraid to approach people. We don't bite. Well, not all of us. You'll find that a lot of your classmates have a lot in common with you. That's how I got through freshman year. Well, that and finding this slab of man meat next to me!"

"Aww, babe, you're embarrassing me," Eddie said coyly.

"I'll keep that in mind. The whole friends thing, I mean," Will said.

"Good," Krystal said.

Just then, the car pulled up to the entrance gate of Presley Place. Eddie reached out to enter the code to open the gate and then proceeded inward. Will wanted to look out of the window on the opposite side to see what numbers Eddie had inputted, but the football gear obstructed his view. Will gave him the directions leading to his house on Penley Avenue. The car pulled up to the curb of Will's house.

As Will exited the vehicle, Krystal rolled down her window to address Will once more. "You ever need advice or anything, we're around." Krystal rolled back up her window, and the car drove off.

When Will entered the house, he saw DeMarcus standing by the windows in the barely used dining room area, looking through the open blinds. "Yo, who was that? She was fine! And she had that good hair too?!" DeMarcus asked.

"That was Krystal. She gave me a ride home. Well, she and her boyfriend did."

"That goofy lookin' white boy pushin' that busted-down hoopty is her boyfriend?!"

"Yup."

"Man, I can't believe it! They out here takin' all our sistas! It's a shame!"

"Really?" Will asked sarcastically.

"Yeah, it is. Tell me why they wanna go for the white meat when they got fine bruthas they can be choosin' from? I'm talkin' 'bout me of course; I don't know 'bout you. I'm still tryin' to figure out who in the family you got your ugly from."

"Tell me, DeMarcus. All those girls you got numbers from yesterday, were they all black?"

"I mean…some of them was…one of them was…Alright, the rest was white girls. But it's different for me 'cuz…'cuz…uh… Man, shut up! Dang, you stay hatin'!" DeMarcus shouted to the other end of the house, "Mama, Will in here hatin' again! You want me to go get the belt?!

Will ignored DeMarcus and walked to the staircase. Before he placed one foot on a stair, he was approached by his mother. She was carrying a large basket of clean clothes from the laundry room behind the kitchen.

"You're home a bit late, aren't you?" Liz asked Will.

"Uh…yeah," Will answered. "I, uh…joined the Booster Club."

Liz immediately dropped the basket onto the floor and gasped with joy. "Oh, honey! I'm so proud of you! I knew you would want to get involved in things sooner or later!" At no time did Liz inquire as to what the Booster Club was or what Will did as a member of it. Instead, she wrapped her arms around his stomach, giving him the most motherly bear hug possible and refusing to let go. "Um…yeah…thanks," Will said, struggling to breathe.

Liz released her grip on Will and said, "Well, dinner is in the fridge if you're ready to eat."

"What is it?" Will asked.

Liz's smile went from sincere to false as she answered, "Why, it's the same thing you had yesterday and the day before; free food. Do you need to know anything else?"

"No, ma'am," he said. "But I should probably get started on this homework first. I'll come back down in a minute and eat."

Will retreated to his room and began his homework, reading the assigned pages of Arthur Miller's play *The Crucible* and answering the questions based on it given to him on a worksheet. Without pro wrestling on TV to distract him, he was about five percent more committed to his schoolwork than he was yesterday. Will was able to complete the worksheet, answering questions about deeper meanings and what messages the author was trying to convey with certain passages in the text. At that point, his mind had joined his body in total fatigue; he was done for the day. Will stretched his entire body across his bed, covering as much of the bed as possible as he closed his eyes.

***

Gray clouds eclipsed the sun and the blue skies, and an ominous wind filled the atmosphere. There didn't seem to be anyone around for miles, save for an eleven-year-old William sitting on a swing alone wearing a black hoodie. There should have been another swing beside him, but it was gone; the seat and the binding chains were nowhere to be found.

The young Will looked down at the ground as his hands gripped the chains of the swing. "I don't think she's coming to talk today," he said, still looking down. "I don't think she'll be here tomorrow, either. Or the day after." Will looked back up and behind him. "I don't think she's ever going to talk with us again. She's gone for good."

The winds grew stronger, and the skies grew darker. "She would still be here, you know, if she would've just listened to us. Did what we asked and left us alone. Either way, we'd still be here sitting by ourselves."

The sky was now entirely dark as the wind continued to blow. The younger Will and the swing he was sitting on were the only visible objects in the vicinity. "We're meant to be alone, William. Nothing or no one can change that. It doesn't matter what we do. And it certainly doesn't matter where we go. This is our inescapable fate: to live this life alone. Remember that, and no one will else have to suffer. We won't have to suffer." At that moment, the young Will faded into the pitch black environment.

Chapter Eight

The light of the dawning sun shone through the barely opened blinds of the windows of Will's room. Will lay across his bed with his eyes wide open. He had been in this state for at least an hour, not moving once. Only two days into high school, and so much weighed heavily on his mind: the events that had been taking place, the people he'd encountered, and especially the visions, voices, and nightmares that had played on an unending loop in his head. All of these things started to take their toll on Will. It affected him physically as well as mentally. He ate far less than normal, and he didn't get nearly as much sleep as he used to. Will wished he could completely turn off his mind and lie in bed like this for the entire day. However, the small alarm clock on the top of the dresser next to his bed denied him his request.

"W-W-W-Wake up, Ingram Park! It's ya boy Captain Crunch, and I got the Wakeup Crew with me!"

"Yo yo, it's your boy Skizzle from the South Side!"

"And you know we got DJ Crust on the ones and twos for your morning mix!"

"You're tuned into the dopest morning show on the radio! Only here on 98.5 The Heat, blazing Ingram Park with the hottest hip-hop and R&B!"

"It's time for WAKE AND BAKE WITH SKIZZLE AND CAPTAIN CRUNCH! Only here on THE HEAT!"

"Yo, Skizz!"

"What's happening, Captain?"

"Say, man, what you think about this Y2K everybody's talking about?"

"I ain't worried about it. Y2K ain't nothin' compared to when the machines come get us."

"Man, you been watching that movie again? What is this, like, the tenth time?"

"I'm tellin ya', Captain, that ain't no movie. That's a documentary, based on real life. When you gonna take the red pill and accept that?"

"Yeah, alright, Skizzle. I'll believe ya when you start jumping buildings, dodging bullets, and bending spoons. You buggin', man, real talk. I ain't worried 'bout no machines, and I ain't sweatin' no Y2K. I'm smart wit' it. I took all my ends out the ATM and stashed it in the couch at my mama house. And you know what? Caller number nine with the phrase that pays? Imma give ya ninety-eight dollars and fifty cents of it. Start your hump day off right, only here on WAKE AND BAKE!

"And keep it locked here 'cuz we got your hookup on the biggest show of the year! That's right, I'm talkin' 'bout FRIDAY

FREAKFEST '99, live from the Palisades Center in Fremont! We just got word that DMX will be performing!"

Will sprung up and turned off his alarm clock. He had had about all he could take from the two loud radio personalities and their reminder that his day had begun, whether he wanted it to or not. Sitting up on his bed, he rubbed his eyes, which were red from lack of sleep.

Will went through the motions when it came to his morning hygiene regimens. Compared to his brother, who prioritized his looks over almost everything else, Will's time in the bathroom was brief. Furthermore, whereas his brother would take an abundant amount of time coordinating the outfit he'd wear for the day, Will would throw on one of the many similar pairs of blue jeans he owned, a basic black T-shirt, and one of his hoodies over it. Of course, sometimes he would change up his wardrobe. Today, for example, Will wore a light grey hoodie rather than the blue one he'd been wearing.

With his backpack in his hand and his CD player in his hoodie pockets, Will went downstairs to be greeted by his parents and his sister who were already awake and prepared for their day. They were all sitting around the table. Anthony was reading the paper, while Liz sat beside Rosetta helping her with her times tables for school.

"Morning," Will greeted the three in a lackadaisical tone.

"Good morning to you, too. Are you okay? You look half-dead," Liz said with a concerned look.

Will grumbled, "I'm fine. Just didn't get as much sleep as I would've liked to."

"Well, sit down and have some breakfast. There's still some Fiber One cereal in the pantry. Or you've got time to make some turkey sausage with egg whites."

None of those things sounded appealing in the least to Will. "No thanks," he said.

"Will, you have to eat something. I noticed that your plate from last night is still wrapped up in the refrigerator."

"I wasn't hungry."

Anthony folded his newspaper, placed it down on the table, and chimed in, "So, you're not eating and you're not sleeping? You on that stuff, boy?"

"What stuff?" Will asked.

"You know what stuff I'm talking about, boy. You smoking that Mary Jane? You sniffing that coke? You doing that um… that… What's the thing the kids are doing today? You know, Liz. The one that was on the news last night with the kids and they were wearing all those goofy color clothes and sucking on those pacifiers like they're still babies? Euphoria!"

"Ecstasy, honey," Liz corrected.

"Yeah, that! You doin' that?!"

"No, sir," Will said.

"Better not be. I ain't spending no money for you to go to rehab. I'll just whip that behind until you don't even wanna talk about drugs anymore."

"You're the one who started talking about drugs, Dad."

"That ain't the point. See, Liz, talking back to parents. That's another sign."

"Missus Honey says drugs are bad, and we should just say no," Rosetta added to the conversation.

"That's right!" Anthony exclaimed. "You listen to Mrs. Honey!"

"I gotta go," Will said.

"This early?" Liz asked.

"Yes, ma'am. I'm meeting a friend. See you later."

"You better not be meeting them to smoke that reefer!" Anthony shouted to Will who was already at the front door.

"Anthony, stop!" Liz said. "Have a good day, honey!" Liz shouted to Will. However, Will couldn't hear her over the beeping of the security alarm as he exited the house. "Where are you going?" Liz asked Anthony, who had gotten up from the table. "Gonna check that boy's drawers for drugs."

"He is not on drugs! You know that he's been having a hard time dealing with…you know what."

Anthony sat back down. "Yeah, I know," he said defeated. "Where is that other boy at?! Isn't his bus coming in five minutes?"

Will started his walk to school. He left home earlier than he had yesterday. The sun was still rising, and the sky was still a bit dark. There weren't any kids standing at the bus stop, Nathan included, so Will was relieved knowing that he'd be able to walk in peace. He put in the earbuds and turned on the CD player. His walk would go uninterrupted and undisturbed, and for a moment, Will was optimistic. If this peaceful walk was any indication, he believed that today was going to be a cakewalk.

That was until he reached the corner of Benbrook and Chisholm. The long, loud scream of "DUUUUUUUDE!"

broke through the music from Will's earbuds. Will took off his earbuds, turned around and saw Nathan running towards him from the convenience store with a plastic bag in one hand and his skateboard cuffed in his other arm. Will remained at the corner, allowing Nathan to catch up.

Nathan took a few seconds to catch his breath. "What's up, dude?" Nathan asked, still breathing heavily.

"Don't 'What's up, dude' me!" Will said angrily. The two started to walk to school together. "What the hell was that yesterday?"

"What are you talking about?"

"The library. That girl Ashley. What was that even about?"

"Oh, yeah. I probably should've warned ya, dude. There is, like, no subtlety with that girl. She wanted to see how much of yourself you were willing to reveal off the bat."

"What?!"

"Sorry, dude. That's kinda Ashley Baker's thing. She's a really smart girl. It's her thing to want to know everything she possibly can about things and people. But she has a very eccentric way about getting information, especially when she's face-to-face with people. If I had to guess, she wasn't completely sure how to approach you at first."

"Hmm…"

"Look, dude. All I'm saying is, don't be quick to dismiss her, okay? I don't think she sees you as just some experiment or whatever. She's genuinely interested in you. Hell, I'd wager that wants to be your friend. Which his rare for her; trust me, I know."

"And what if I don't want to be hers? Sorry, Nathan, but I'm not so keen on the whole 'friendship' thing right now."

"Well, aren't we edgy? That's a shame dude, because that's lesson two of suburban life: Never walk alone. There're some vicious people roaming our fair campus. People known for sniffing out easy prey and feeding on them. And prey doesn't come any easier than a lone guppy in a sea full of sharks."

Before Will knew it, the two boys were standing in front of the quad area of Washington High. Will sighed heavily and said to Nathan, "Fine, I'll give her another chance."

"Aw, sweet, dude," Nathan said with a look of excitement and satisfaction. "Here, take this." Nathan gave Will a plastic bag with a blueberry muffin wrapped in plastic inside. Will took his hands out of his pockets and took the bag with both of them.

"What am I supposed to do with this?" Will asked.

"I think you know, dude," Nathan answered. "I'd give it to her myself, but I gotta go deliver some homework to Caitlyn before homeroom." With a huge grin he finished, "She said she would let me carry her books to class if I did…I mean…helped her with her homework. That's just stage one, dude!"

Nathan walked off while Will remained stationary for another minute. He looked down into the plastic bag he was holding. "Do people really want to be friends with me? Am I even capable of having friends?" he asked himself with severe doubt. Will looked back up to the highly populated quad and walked through the campus to the library building.

The library was as empty as it had been yesterday. Will started to wonder if anyone actually visited the library at any time during the day. Will spotted Ashley occupying the table with the computers by herself. He approached her and tapped on her shoulder.

Without turning around at first, Ashley answered, "You're early." She turned around and was shocked to see that it was Will, instead of Nathan, greeting her. "Oh! I didn't think I'd see you again anytime soon."

Will reached into the plastic bag and handed her the muffin. "Sorry about yesterday. I shouldn't have yelled at you like that."

Ashley reluctantly took the muffin. "You didn't poison this, did you?"

"What?! Why would I do that?"

Ashley chuckled. "Just kidding. You don't have to apologize, though. It was my fault. Nathan's always telling me not to dig so deep. But I can't help it sometimes. It's in my nature to want to know everything." Ashley began to eat the muffin.

Satisfied that they were on more or less moderate terms with each other, Will started to walk away. "Okay then. I will see you around," he said hesitantly.

"WAIT!" Ashley shouted as best she could with bits of muffin still in her mouth.

Will stopped and watched Ashley quickly finish the remainder of the muffin. She asked, "Wanna see what I do to stave off boredom? Come here and check this out."

Will took the chair next to Ashley. He leaned in to look at her computer screen. He saw a white screen full of words, words that he normally knew the meaning to, but in this particular context, he was ignorant. "What am I looking at?" he asked.

Without pause, Ashley began to explain. "What you're looking at is code. This is what makes the programs on your computer work. And this is what I like to do. I write programs, and I'm damn good at it, too, if I say so myself. This particular program only took about five days and thirty-two blueberry muffins to write, a personal record."

"What does it do?"

"Glad you asked. Washington High gets its internet from the biggest ISP in the area, TeleTronic, a subsidiary of the Taylor Corporation. TeleTronic also dabbles in phone and, more importantly, cellular phone service. In a way that would be impossible to explain without the aid of a white board and some coloring books, their cell phone service and internet service work on the same infrastructure; they're kinda intertwined with one another. My program, when run from a computer on the school's internet connection, allows me to intercept text messages from any cell phone on the TeleTronic network that are sent or received on campus and displays those texts right here without anyone knowing."

"Uh huh," Will said. He only understood about forty-five percent of what Ashley was explaining. "And why would you do this?"

"Two reasons," Ashley answered. "First, major corporations always hire people like me to find flaws, bugs, and vulnerabilities in their networks. Vulnerabilities that would allow hackers to do…well, exactly what I'm doing. Then they pay us huge lumps of cash to write programs that fix 'em. Second, and most importantly, this way, I find out all the big things that are going down here at Washington; anything from who's dating who to who stashed a dead body in the trunk of their car last summer and made their friends swear a blood oath not to tell anyone about it. And all without having to snoop around the old-fashioned way. It's why I run it on a computer at the library instead of the computer lab. No one ever suspects anyone of using these outdated things for anything other than…say, email…at the most."

Admittedly, Will became more interested in Ashley's project the more she explained it. "Say, Ashley. Could you look up a certain name or word in those text messages? To see if anyone mentions it?"

"Hmmm. Wanna see if anyone's talking about you? If anyone's crushing on you?"

"I doubt that anyone would even know who I am, let alone waste a text message regarding me. Yesterday I overheard two boys mention 'F2' and that there would be an announcement about it tonight. They weren't allowed to talk about it in public for some reason."

"OOOH!" Ashley said with excitement. "That's what I'm talking about! This could be huge! Tell you what. I've got CompSci first period. I'll modify the code to include a search query function. Then we can run a search on this 'F2' and see what it's about."

It was about time for the homeroom bell to ring, so Will got up from the chair and grabbed his backpack. The next thing he wanted to say was, "I'll see you later," confirming a new bond with Ashley, but before he could open his mouth to form the words, a very loud alarm buzzed from the intercoms. As the alarm continued to sound, Will asked Ashley, "IS THAT THE FIRE ALARM?!"

Highly annoyed at the silence penetrating alarm, Ashley answered, "NO! SOMETHING FAR CRAPPIER!"

***

The air was filled with tension all the students stood next to their lockers. School security officers armed to the teeth from head to toe patrolled up and down the hallway. The officers carried leashes tied to the German shepherds tasked with detecting illegal substances. The officers patted down students at random, while the dogs took sniffs at each locker. As one boy was being forcefully patted down, the girl next to him bent down to pet the officer's dog. "Who's the most adorable thing in the world? You are!" she said to the dog in a cutesy tone.

Further down the hall, Will stood with his hands in his pockets and one foot pressed against his locker. He had but a few words to sum up his observation of this situation: "A whole lot of red paint." Next to him, a girl stood by her locker panicked and sweating profusely. It took a second, but Will recognized her as the girl from the group who loitered at the convenience store.

"This is just great," the girl said to herself. "Gee, thanks for giving me a ride and making sure I went to school today, Mom.

Oh, and, Casey, I am so glad you asked ME to stash the stuff! Oh crap, here they come!"

An officer made his way to Will's and the girl's lockers, and her fears became reality. The accompanying dog snarled and then let out loud barks.

"Open it," the officer said with threatening authority. But his demand wasn't directed to the girl; it was to Will. Will was surprised at first. Without protest, he pushed himself away from the locker and proceeded to open it. The dog sniffed through Will's locker for a few minutes, but wasn't able to track the source of the smell that had previously caught its attention.

Another officer joined the one at Will's locker. "What's up?" she asked.

"The dog caught a whiff of something, but now he can't trace it," the first officer answered.

"Hmph, these kids nowadays are always coming up with new ways to hide their stuff. They think they're clever. This one probably hid his mule-style. Nonetheless, take him and get an UA sample."

"Roger. Let's go, kid."

The officer grabbed Will by the arm and led him to the nearby restroom. Will looked back and noticed the girl that was by the locker beside his breathing a huge sigh of relief as the other officers moved on to continue their searches. The officer shoved Will into the restroom. Near the sinks, another officer stood with a cart with sealed round plastic containers, some of which were full. "Got another one for you," the officer who escorted Will to the restroom said. The monitor gave Will one of the empty containers and demanded, "Fill it to the red line."

Will walked into one of the empty stalls being monitored by the officer by the sink. He proceeded to fill the cup as demanded when he heard the voice of Rob who was occupying the stall next to his. "Hey, you know I can't pee with you standing there lookin' at me! I got that PPS, homie! Man, turn around or somethin'!" The officer didn't buy into Rob's ailment. "Hurry up and fill the cup, Robert. I've got a feeling other people are going to need to use that stall."

Will, on the other hand, completely filled his cup. He walked out of the stall, handed the officer the cup and started washing his hands. "Hey, Officer Warren, lemme ask you somethin'," Rob said from his stall.

"What, Robert?" the officer responded, growing more annoyed.

"At what point in your life did you say to yourself, 'Ya know, I really want a job where I can watch teenage boys use the bathroom?' Where did all go wrong for you?"

Officer Warren ran the test on Will's sample. "Yeah, keep it up, Stanley. We'll see how funny you are when you're on a bus heading to juvenile hall."

"Tch. Man, juvie can't hold me! I'm BIG ROB, DAWG!" Once again, Rob let out loud barking noises. Then, he walked out of the stall and handed his sample to Officer Warren. "Here, take your sample. Look at your life, homie. This the highlight of your whole week, looking at pee! How sad are you right now?"

Officer Warren took Rob's sample and began testing it as he did Will's before.

"Yo, what's up, Willy Will?!" Rob asked Will. Rob extended his hand anticipating a high five. But Will gave him a disgusted look.

"Oh, snap!" Rob said, realizing his mistake. He started washing his hands. As he rubbed the soap on his hands in the running water, he asked Will, "Can you believe Five-O runnin' up on us like this, homie? Singling us out like we got all kind of priors and warrants. You know what this is, right? This ain't nothing but racism right here. Another instance of the white man holdin' us bruthas down!"

Before Will could answer Rob, Officer Warren interjected. "You're clean. Head to your homeroom and await the bell," he said to Will. He then looked at Rob with much chagrin. "You're clean too, Stanley. Head to your homeroom."

"Yeah, whatever you say, pig," Rob answered.

Chapter Nine

The bell rang, transitioning second period to third. Will walked back to the E building to his locker. With his hands in his pockets again, he looked around as he walked, looking out for security officers as if he had something to hide. Will opened his locker and replaced the textbook he needed for second period for the one he needed for the third. After grabbing the textbook, he closed the door to his locker to be greeted once again by the girl in the white dress. Will didn't look at her at first; he stared directly in front of his locker and said to himself, "Not really in the mood for this."

The girl laughed. Will turned his head to address her and asked, "What's so funny?"

"There you go again. Always focusing on the negative, not seeing the positive," she answered.

"What positive?" Will asked. "Where were you when they dragged me from my locker and forced me to pee into a cup? Where was the positive in that?" He started looking around, once again looking for security officers. "You gonna be around when someone catches me out here talking to myself and swears I'm on drugs?"

"Probably not," she responded as she giggled. "But your friends will be."

"My friends?" Will asked

"Yeah, dude, your friends. What's up?"

The girl was gone. In her place stood Nathan and Ashley, startling Will. "Did you guys see a girl in white standing here?"

"Um…no," Ashley answered. "Are you okay?"

"Yeah, dude, you're not on that stuff, are you?" Nathan added.

"I'm not on drugs!" Will exclaimed, tired of the accusations. "Never mind. How'd you know this is where my locker was?" He asked.

"I looked up your info in the student database," Ashley answered.

"How did you do…you know what? Never mind. What are y'all doing here?"

"We wanted to grab you before they made the announcement. We didn't want you to leave without us, dude," Nathan responded.

"What announcement?" Will asked.

Ashley looked down at the wristwatch on her left arm and said, "The one they're about to make in about five seconds."

Her prediction was correct. In exactly five seconds from her saying so, a chime was heard from the nearby intercom:

"Attention, students of Washington High, this is Principal Caine speaking. Apparently, according to one of your classmates' team of high priced lawyers, this morning's impromptu drug search was a 'blatant violation of your civil liberties'. So, while I sort this mess out and hopefully prevent a lengthy lawsuit, I've been instructed by the district superintendent to cancel the remainder of today's classes, along with all extracurricular activities. You are all to leave the campus as soon as possible and in an organized and disciplined manner. Also, as a reminder, tickets for Friday's game are still on sale. You may purchase them in the administration building tomorrow. Not today, tomorrow. That is all."

Another chime rang from the intercom. The hallways began to flood with students preparing to leave campus.

Will started to ask, "How did you know that…"

"Who cares, dude? Let's get outta here!" Nathan interrupted with the utmost excitement.

The three walked side by side as they left the Washington High campus. The senior parking lot and school bus area was chaotic as the seniors who drove caused a traffic jam trying to leave, and legions of other students stood in one central area waiting for the buses to arrive. Will, Ashley, and Nathan, along with a few other students, left the school from its front entrance, immediately turning left on the sidewalk towards Chisholm Road.

"So, dudes, what are we doing with all this free time? I say we go to the mall. You know, since there are going to be way more hot girls now than ever," Nathan said as the trio walked.

"Go to sleep and forget today happened?" Will suggested.

"We're going to your house," Ashley insisted.

"Aw, that's lame, dude. Why my house?" Nathan complained.

"I need to use your computer."

"What's wrong with yours? You didn't bust it trying to, I don't know, hack into the Pentagon or something did ya?"

"Nothing's wrong with mine. I just can't get to it right now because…" Ashley blushed a bit in embarrassment before she admitted, "I forgot my house key again."

Nathan laughed as loud as he possibly could while Ashley grumbled.

"Okay, we can all hang out at my house for a while," Nathan said. He then pointed at the convenience store. "But first, check it out. Is that a Tasty Pastries truck pulling into the gas station?"

Ashley gasped and then blurted out with glee, "They're restocking the blueberry muffins!" She started to run towards the convenience store, leaving the two boys behind.

Will and Nathan arrived at the convenience store about five minutes later. Rather than joining Ashley inside the store, the two waited outside near the entrance. Will stood against the large window pane next to the large icebox with his hands in his pockets, while Nathan attempted stationary tricks with his skateboard along the curb.

"Check this one out, dude," Nathan said to Will with each attempt. He was able to pull off some of the tricks he attempted. The others he failed spectacularly, falling on the pavement either face-first or tail-first at times. However, each time he fell, he quickly got back on his feet, with no indication that he was injured.

Three minutes later, the two were accompanied by the usual group of the store's teenage loiterers, including Charity, the girl who stood next to Will during the drug search from earlier. Each of them reeked of the smell the drug-sniffing dogs were tasked with detecting.

"'Sup, dudes?" Nathan greeted.

"We were just gonna grab some munchies. Then we're hitting up the skate park," one of the boys answered. "You two down?"

"Can't. Gotta help Ashley with something," Nathan said.

"God, I can't believe you still hang out with her. She's gotta be, like, the biggest lame in Ingram Park," Charity replied.

"Hey, what can I say? Friends for life. Call me a sucker, but I stick with mines no matter what," Nathan rebutted.

Ashley walked out the store holding a bag full of blueberry muffins while eating one. Charity looked at Ashley and then said to Nathan, "Hmph, I figured you would've learned a lesson from what went down last year. But hey, if you wanna be a loser your entire life, that's on you."

Ashley swallowed the remainder of the muffin she was eating. In a confrontational tone, she said to her, "Be sure to thank mommy and daddy's lawyers for getting us out of school early today, Charity."

"How did you know that it was my—"Charity began to ask, but Ashley didn't stick around to answer. She walked towards Benbrook Street with Will and Nathan following behind. Charity stood amongst her group, embarrassed as the other members looked at her. "What? You think I'm some kind of… Shut up, and let's go!" she said.

"But what about the munchies?" one of the boys asked.

"Hey, I bet they've got some nice snacks at the law firm," said another boy, mocking Charity.

"They actually do," Charity admitted with shame.

"Slow down, Ash!" Nathan shouted as he and Will ran to catch up to her. Ashley walked at an accelerated pace with a look of disgust on her face.

"How dare she bring *that* back up?!" Ashley asked after Nathan and Will finally caught up to her.

"Calm down, dude," Nathan said. "Remember, no matter what, *she's* gone for good, and she ain't never comin' back. What's past is past."

Although Nathan's words were directed at Ashley, who received them with relief, they resonated with Will as well. "You're right. Now let's hurry to your house. If I unglue my eyes from a computer screen for too long…" She widened her eyes and leaned into Will with an eerie look, "I tend to get crazy."

Will gasped in fear. Nathan and Ashley, on the other hand, shared a laugh for a few seconds.

"C'mon, dudes," Nathan said afterwards.

The trio continued their walk to Presley Place. As they walked on the sidewalk on Benbrook Street, Ashley tapped away on her cell phone while the boys engaged in a heavy debate.

"No way in hell, dude! There's no way the awesome, super badass team of Bill Goldberg, Eddie Guerrero, Booker T, Scott Steiner, and Diamond Dallas Page is gonna lose to…to…who was in your team of scrubs again?"

"Kurt Angle, Steve Blackman, Hardcore Holly, The Godfather, and The Big Show. In a classic Survivor Series Five-On-Five match."

"Yeah, dude. We'll take that victory with only two wrestlers on our side being pinned or submitted. It'll prove once and for all that WCW's the superior promotion."

"If you say so."

"I'm serious, dude. WCW's gonna be around forever, and I promise you a whole lot more of your guys are gonna jump ship soon."

"You think?"

"Dude, I know! In fact, I will eat my own underwear if any of the guys on my team end up working for Vince."

Ashley placed her cell phone back into her pocket and intervened in Will and Nathan's debate. "You two know that stuff's fake, right? My God, is that all you boys talk about? Butts and pro wrestling?

"No," Nathan answered defensively. "We talk about real important stuff, too. Like, like politics! Like you know? Al Gore and Pat Buchanan…"

Will added, "And which one of them would win in a steel cage match on pay-per-view."

Ashley laughed. "If you two say so."

The three kids reached the front gate of Presley Place. Nathan approached the keypad that would open the gate and entered the correct code. As he did, Will leaned in to see what numbers Nathan inputted for future reference. The gate opened, and the three entered the housing community.

Nathan's house was two streets further down from Will's. It was one of the few one-story homes in the entire neighborhood. With it being sandwiched between two larger houses and trees surrounding both sides of its lawn, it was a bit hard to see it. The three made their way inside the Stone residence and towards Nathan's room towards the back.

Nathan's room was standard fare for a teenage boy. The wall was almost entirely covered in posters featuring rock bands, movies, and bikini models. Clothes poured out of his closet in a pile on the ground and shoes lay everywhere around the room. As Nathan entered, he kicked things around, giving Will and Ashley a clear path in which to walk. Will sat on the red bean bag chair beside Nathan's bed, and Ashley sat at the wooden desk across from it.

Ashley powered on the computer. A few minutes later, she connected to the Internet to check her email. "Ah! C'mon, man! That's so gross!" she screamed in disgust in response to what was displayed on the screen after a few keystrokes.

"Had I known you were coming over, I would've cleared my browsing history," Nathan responded nonchalantly.

Ashley got up from the chair.

"Where are you going?" Nathan asked.

She answered, "To get some disinfectant or something. I think I'm going to be sick." She left the room.

"So Will, I see ya always carrying around that CD player," Nathan said.

"Yeah, so?"

"So, what do you listen to?"

"Mostly hip-hop. A bit of rock and some dance music."

"Cool, cool. But tell me. Do you like…" Nathan grabbed a remote from in between the covers of his unmade bed. He pressed the play button that powered his stereo and finished his question, "DEATH METAL?!" Loud guitar riffs and the bang of drums blared from the tall speakers. Shortly after, the loud, shrieking voice of the vocalist rang from the speakers. Will had no clue as to what he was saying.

Having to raise his voice to a level louder than the music, Will asked, "What is this?!"

Nathan answered, "This is Subverted Repulsion! They're East Germany's most hardcore metal band! This is their newest LP, *Derivative Annihilation!* Cost me extra 'cuz I had to get the record store to import it for me!"

"Why?!"

"'Cuz they're banned in the U.S., dude! You sacrifice one squirrel on stage to the blood gods, and everyone gets all pissy about it!"

The song playing started a guitar solo. Nathan leapt on the bed and started head banging while pretending to play guitar. "Dude! I need to be in a band! Band guys get all the groupies!" Nathan said.

"I hear Jessie's still looking for a bass player!" Ashley said standing in the doorway.

"Screw her, dude! She totally c-blocked me a few weeks ago!" Nathan rebutted.

"Now who has the problem letting go? What's past is past, right?"

Ashley walked back to the computer. She sprayed the disinfectant onto the keyboard and mouse and wiped both down with a paper towel. She sat back down and tossed the used paper towel into the nearby trash basket.

Will sat on the bean bag and continued to watch Nathan furiously head bang to the music. He shifted his head a bit to the opposite side. Sitting on the edge of the bed was the girl in the white dress. She was bobbing her head left and right to the music. When she noticed that Will was looking at her, she smiled and shrugged her shoulders. Will gasped in shock, but neither Ashley nor Nathan could hear him because of the music. He did a double take. He looked back at Nathan and then back at the edge of the bed. The girl was gone.

Meanwhile, Ashley, who had finished another muffin, inserted a zip disk into the computer's disk drive. It contained the program she had spoken to Will about earlier. The music was still playing as loud as before, so the three still had to shout to make sure they heard each other. "Hey, Will! Come check this out!" Ashley said.

Will got up from his bean bag chair and joined Ashley at the computer. He asked, "What's up?"

Ashley explained, "I took your advice and added a search function to the program! Then I ran a search for that 'F2' you mentioned and archived the results!" Ashley pressed a key on the keyboard to load the archive. A large list of text messages populated the screen. "That's just from first and second period! A lot of people are talking about this 'F2' thing! But they texted about it in a discreet manner."

Will read some of the archived texts to himself. Ashley was correct. The texts didn't make sense. Some of them read like "Got spot picked for F2" and "Gonna get them on F2."

Ashley continued, "This is the kinda stuff I'm looking for! Whether you wanted to or not, you stumbled onto something big! We need to figure out what this 'F2' is!"

"They said they were going to announce something about it tonight! Can you keep searching for it then?!"

"Afraid not! This program is only capable of working on a small scale. If I run it at home, it will document text messages from everybody in Ingram Park using TeleTronic phones. It'll crash for sure! That's why I run it on campus! But if it's going down, I have a feeling more students will be texting about it at school tomorrow!"

Meanwhile, Nathan continued head banging to the music still blasting from the speakers. He started reciting the lyrics along with the song:

"AND THE WORLD WILL TURN!

AND THE PEOPLE WILL LEARN!

AND THE SOCIETY WILL BURRRRRN!"

Just then, the music suddenly turned off. A voice came from near the stereo, "Shouldn't you kids still be in school?"

Nathan bounced off of his bed. "Oh hey, Dad!"

Chapter Ten

The three kids directed their attention to Nathan's dad. There stood a rather tall and muscular man, dressed in a BDU. His hair was as black as Nathan's was, and his face was entirely covered in stubble. The stubble failed to cover the various wrinkles across his face from the years of stress that came with both work and life. Nathan's dad repeated his question, "Why aren't you kids in school right now?"

"They let us out early due to a drug search violating our civil rights or something," Nathan answered.

"Civil liberties," Ashley corrected.

"Yeah, that," Nathan said.

Nathan's dad shook his head. "What's wrong with this country?" he asked. Then he pointed at Will and asked, "Who's he?"

"This is Will," Nathan answered. "He's new to town, kinda. So me and Ash are showin' him the ropes."

Nathan's dad introduced himself to Will. "Colonel Lucas Stone, United States Army." He extended his hand out to Will.

Will rose from his bean bag chair and shook his hand. This was the first person whose hand he shook. "Um…nice to meet you, sir," Will said nervously.

"Likewise," Lucas responded. His handshake was so firm that Will had to rub his hand afterward to soothe the sore feeling he had.

"Hey, Dad, I thought you were out in the woods or something overseeing some super-secret training," Nathan said to his father.

Lucas answered, "Eh, one of the soldiers shattered his knee in several places. So the higher-ups called off the whole training exercise. I swear, this whole country's going soft on me." Nathan's dad continued, "But since you kids are all here, and I don't feel like cooking, I'll order us some pizzas." He pointed at Nathan and said, "I know you like pepperoni." Then he pointed at Ashley and said, "And you like chicken on yours." Finally, he addressed Will asking, "What do you take on yours?"

Will answered, "Beef sausage and banana peppers."

"Banana peppers?" Lucas asked.

Before Will could answer, Lucas continued, "Dear Lord, I swear this country is going to Hell in a handbasket." He pulled out a cellular phone from his pants pocket and walked out of the room as he made the call to the pizza restaurant.

Some time passed. Will, Ashley, and Nathan joined Lucas around the medium-sized, circular, wooden table in the kitchen.

Lucas grasped a small glass half-full of bourbon and looked at the watch on his opposite arm. "Pizza should be here in five more minutes, or it'll be free. They still do that?" he asked. He then grabbed the bottle of Jim Beam from on top of a stack of unopened letters on the table and refilled his glass.

"Now Will, as Nathan's little friend, you'll always be a guest in this house, just like Ashley," Lucas said. "But I have to lay down some ground rules. And by 'rules,' I mean rule, as in one. I don't care if you break anything, it can be replaced. I don't care if you throw wild parties here, it's what you teenagers do. Hell, you can sneak into my liquor cabinet, just don't let me catch you, or I'll have to do the whole 'parent' thing and I don't wanna do that. But so help me, God, if I find out you've eaten even one of the Sunshine Scout cookies I keep in the freezer, I. Will. Destroy. You. Gonna be like Desert Storm all over again in here!"

Will's eyes widened in fear as sweat rolled down his face. The doorbell rang, and Will jumped out of his chair.

Lucas smiled and said, "That must be the pizzas. I'll get 'em." He left to the front door.

Will remained in a state of shock over Lucas' words to him.

Nathan said to him, "Ya know, to be fair, dude, those things are like five bucks a box, and they only sell 'em once a year."

Will eventually recovered from his shock as Lucas returned to the kitchen holding four large boxes of pizza from the local pizza restaurant.

Lucas took a whiff of the aroma coming from the top of the boxes and boasted, "Ah, Giuseppe's! If any of you know of a better pizza joint in town, you'd be wise to keep it to yourself!"

Lucas circled around the table, handing each of the kids a box of the pizza with the toppings they requested. "Okay, here's pepperoni for Nate, chicken for Ash, and beef sausage and… urgh…banana peppers for Will."

The kids began eating the pizza. Still standing up, Lucas finished off the bourbon from his glass and then went to the freezer to replace the ice cubes in the glass. He sat back down, refilled his glass once again, and grabbed a slice of his pizza.

"You know, a lot of people my age say you kids have it lucky these days. I say they're full of it; we had it MUCH easier than you!" Lucas asserted.

"How so?" Nathan asked with a muffled tone as a string of cheese dangled from his mouth.

"Well, take today, for example," Lucas answered. "When I was your age, we didn't have to worry about getting felt up by police officers and sniffed up by dogs like we were jars of peanut butter in school under some guise of 'safety.'"

"No?" Ashley asked.

"Nope," Lucas continued. "In fact, only thing we had to worry about was getting hazed by the older kids. Yeah, every year, some of the juniors and seniors would round up the freshies and do things to 'em, like stuff 'em in lockers and stash 'em in trash cans. Harmless fun, really, especially when it was your time to do the hazin'." He took a large gulp of bourbon from his glass, completely finishing it off. "I ever tell ya, boy? That's how I met your mother."

"No kidding," Nathan said.

"Yup. We had grabbed the same freshie at the same time, and as we dunked him into the trashcan, we looked into each other's eyes and we knew it was love!"

"That so romantic, dude!" Nathan said cheerfully.

"Yeah, well, fast forward a few years, I come home from Kuwait, and I read in the paper that there's a district-wide ban on hazings on account of some kid jumpin' from one of the school buildings 'cuz he 'just couldn't handle it.'" Lucas looked at his now empty glass. He put the glass to the side and reached for the bottle instead. "On a…hic…unrelated note," he said, now drinking directly from the bottle. "That's about the time…our marriage…hic…started goin' downhill."

Will watched in surprise as Lucas's eyes slowly closed and he started to lose control of his words. Lucas slurred as he continued, "But that's beside the point. The hazin's, they had a name. It was a yearly tra…tra…tradition." He took another swig from the bottle. "Wha…wha…what was it called?" he asked. He then leaned back against the chair, "It'll come t…t…to me." Lucas rocked back and forth in his chair so heavily, it almost fell to the floor with him in it.

"Okay, that's enough, old man," Nathan said as he rose from his chair. Nathan walked over to his dad. He lifted Lucas from his chair and placed his arm over his shoulder. Lucas was slouched over Nathan. "Imma go lay him down in his room. I'll be back," Nathan told Will and Ashley.

As Nathan walked towards the back of the house with his inebriated father, a ringing noise came from Ashley's direction.

Ashley reached into her left jeans pocket and retrieved her cell phone. "Hello?" she answered. Ashley rose from the table and walked toward the front door of the house as she continued her phone conversation.

Will, on the other hand, remained at the table. Now he was completely alone as silence filled the kitchen.

"Oh, admit it! This is fun! You're having fun!" A voice spoke out to Will. It was the girl in the white dress once again. Only now, she was sitting across from him in the chair previously occupied by Ashley.

"Am I, now?" Will asked sarcastically. "I don't consider receiving death threats from an alcoholic over Sunshine Scout cookies fun."

"That's all you took from this? Not the free pizza or the fact that you shared it with two people you spent pretty much the entire day with? Two people who consider themselves your friends?"

"Ummm…"

"There you go, looking at only the negative, once again. Keep this up, and you'll never fulfill that promise."

The girl disappeared again, and Will was once again by himself. A few seconds passed, and Will pushed himself away from the table and got up from his chair. He exited the house and joined Ashley outside on the porch area.

The sky was a bit darker than when Will had last seen it; however, the streetlights hadn't kicked on yet. Ashley sat on the top stair of the porch in front of the house while Will stood beside her with his hand in his pockets. "Okay… Love you, too. Bye," she said still on the phone. She pressed the red end button on the phone, placed the phone back into her jeans pocket, and let out a loud angry huff.

"Something wrong?" Will asked, half-interested.

"New York! Can you believe that?!" Ashley responded angrily.

"Ummm…" Will said, not sure what Ashley was referring to.

Ashley explained, "My parents just called and told me they had to take a flight to New York for business ASAP. They didn't even have time to come back home to pack a bag or make sure I wasn't locked out of the house!"

"Sorry to hear that," Will said.

Ashley smiled, "Don't be. Pretty much par for the course now. My parents are top dogs in the Taylor Corporation. They gotta take trips like this all the time. It's the price they pay for us to live comfortably, remember?"

"Right," Will answered.

Just then, Nathan joined the two on the porch. "Okay, the old man's sleeping it off," he said.

Will shifted his focus on Nathan with a slight look of concern. "Oh, don't give me that look, dude. He's not some hardcore drinker, and he ain't never put his hands on me. So there's no need to call child services. He's an excellent father, despite what mom and the courts would have you believe." Nathan responded to Will's concern with a tone that implied he had made this speech several times beforehand.

"Um…okay," Will said.

"My parents aren't coming home anytime soon. You got any more spares?" Ashley asked Nathan changing the conversation.

"Yeah, I think there's a few left in the box, I'll go grab one," Nathan answered. He then went back inside the house.

Without looking back at Will, Ashley heavily patted the area next to her on the stair, inviting him to sit down next to her.

Will accepted her invitation and sat beside her with his hands still in his pockets. For a while, the two didn't talk to each other; Ashley looked towards the dimly lit skies, while Will looked down at the sidewalk that connected the patio to the driveway. A few minutes passed.

Still looking down at the ground, Will asked, "So this is life in the 'burbs?"

"A small part of it, yeah," Ashley answered still looking at the sky.

"It's…uh…not that bad."

"Oh? That never-changing frown on your face led me to assume you thought otherwise."

"Sorry. I don't smile much."

"No need to apologize. Besides, it's not because you're like sad or depressed or anything like that, is it? No, I can tell you've got the look of someone who always has a lot on his mind."

"You don't know the half of it."

Ashley let out a chuckle. "Yeah, well, no matter what it is you're going through, you'll get by with a little help from your friends."

Will looked at Ashley and asked, "Isn't that line from that song on *The Wonder Years?*"

"Is it? Never watched it. What I'm saying is, stick by your friends, your true friends, and they'll help you resolve your issues. Or, at the very least, help you forget they exist for a while."

"And you and Nathan? Are you two…my friends?" Will asked hesitantly.

Ashley tilted her head back down from the sky and answered, "Well, Nate thinks you're cool enough to hang out with us, and even though we might've started off on the wrong foot, you did bring me a blueberry muffin earlier today. So yeah, I'd say we're friends."

Will didn't smile. However, he was happy to hear that. More than happy, he was surprised. Surprised at the fact that all it took to get in Ashley's good graces was a muffin. To him, Ashley didn't seem like much of a people-person; he had thought that she only befriended people she'd spent a lot of time with and could really trust. But no; all it took was a muffin.

Nathan came back outside holding a small key. He handed the key to Ashley and said, "Sorry it took so long. Dad moved the box into the garage. Somebody should clean that place. Anyway, there's about two more keys left after this one; we should get some more copies this weekend."

"Thanks," Ashley said taking the spare key.

Nathan noticed Will and Ashley sitting next to each other on the porch. "Oh I'm sorry. Am I interrupting a special little heart-to-heart between you two?" he asked.

"N-n-no!" Ashley answered bashfully. "I…I was just telling Will that no matter what he's going through, life's easier with friends around."

"Ah! Lesson number three! I was gonna get around to that one. Anyways, it's getting late, and I've got homework to do."

"Your homework? Or Caitlyn's?" Will asked.

"Nah, dude. It's history, so Brandi's. Or is it Stacy's? Whichever one kissed me on the cheek today," Nathan answered with a huge smile. "But before that, c'mon, Ash. I'll walk you home."

Ashley got up from the stair and walked toward the driveway. Nathan joined her. Looking back, he asked Will, "You gonna be okay, dude?"

Will got up and answered, "Yeah, I'll be fine." He joined the two at the driveway. "It was fun hanging out with you guys today. I'll see y'all at school tomorrow."

"Later, dude," Nathan replied.

"Bye, Will," Ashley added.

Nathan and Ashley walked down the street together, while Will put on his earbuds and walked toward his house in the opposite direction.

Will turned onto Presley Place's main road on the way to his house. The music playing through his earbuds drowned out the sounds of the children playing, the cars driving by, and the sprinklers running on various yards. Will's walk was peaceful for a time. However, there was a sound that penetrated through the music. It was the steady beeping sound of a heart monitor. The beeps grew louder and became more rapid in repetition; soon it was the only thing Will could hear. Will paused, took off his earbuds, and placed them back in his pockets, but the fast beeps still buzzed in his ears, drowning out all the sounds the music did before. Even after covering his ears, he couldn't block out the beeping.

Large beads of sweat ran down Will's face as he stood on the sidewalk. As the beeps continued, Will continued his walk at a slower pace than before. The silence between each beep grew smaller and smaller over time, until eventually the constant beeps turned into a single constant flatline sound.

At that moment, with the flatline sound still ringing in his head, Will ran as fast as he could to his house. At the door, Will frantically reached for his house key in his left jeans pocket. His fingers shook as he attempted to open the door. Will finally managed to open the door. The flatline sound was replaced by the beeps of the security alarm.

"William?!" his mother exclaimed from the couch living room.

Will stood pressed against the front door. He wiped the sweat from his face. "Yes, ma'am," he finally answered as he took off his shoes. He walked into the living room to address his mother who was laughing very loudly. She lay across the couch watching television with a strawberry wine cooler in her hand.

"Another late meeting with the Booster Club?" she asked in a manner as casual as her posture upon the couch.

"Yes, ma'am," he answered. He lied, of course, failing to mention the fact that school had let out early and he had spent the rest of the day at Nathan's.

With her free hand she reached over the couch, pointed toward the kitchen and said, "Well there's some dinner in the fridge. It's…"

"I'm going to bed," Will interrupted. He headed to the stairwell.

Liz looked up towards the stairwell and said to Will, "But it's only…" She looked back towards the LED clock on the cable box and then back up, "7:25."

"Good night, Mom," Will replied as he continued his hike upstairs.

Liz did show a genuine look of concern as Will walked upstairs. But then something happened on the television that grabbed her attention, to which she loudly responded, "What are you thinking? Go for the steaks? They're the most expensive!" as she sloshed the wine cooler bottle around. A few seconds later she shouted, "Good night, baby!" up the stairs, but her words didn't reach Will. He was already in his room, sealed behind a closed door.

Chapter Eleven

The sky was pitch black. However, the constant flashes of lightning that filled it illuminated the road. Rain slowly fell from the dark sky but became heavier over time. With one of his hands holding his head up, Will stared into the window at the long strip of road he and a few others were traveling upon.

Sharing the reflection on the rain soaked window was a girl wearing a light pink blouse. She looked in Will's direction with genuine concern. She placed her hand on top of his free hand. However, Will didn't notice the gesture. He continued to stare out the window. He didn't hear the rain outside or the roar of the accompanying thunder. He didn't hear the two teenagers in the front seat talking, nor did he hear the music coming from the radio, nor did he hear the girl beside him call out to him. The only thing Will could hear was…

"Leave him alone!" she cried out to the group of boys that surrounded eight-year-old William. The boys cornered Will near the blue lockers and had spent the last five minutes taunting Will, taking turns shoving him around until he fell to the ground.

Will didn't even attempt to resist the boys in any way, nor did he attempt to escape them. He remained on the ground.

When the girl, also eight-years-old, shouted her demand, the boys shifted her attention to her. One of the boys broke from the circle that enveloped Will to confront the girl.

"What did you say?" he asked in an intimidating manner as he walked closer to her.

Without showing any fear, the girl clenched her fists and repeated her demand, "I said leave him alone."

The boy was toe-to-toe with the girl now. He looked down to stare at her. The girl refused to back down from the boy. He turned his head around to address his friends.

"Hey, y'all. Moon's girlfriend's here to save him!"

One of the other boys mockingly responded, "Oh, no, y'all, we better get up outta here! We don't wanna catch a beatdown from her!"

The other boys started laughing as the first boy rejoined them.

"Getting saved by a girl? Man, Moon, you're so pathetic. It's ain't even fun messin' with you," the first boy said, shaking his head.

The group dispersed from around Will and walked away. The girl walked to Will and bent down to help him up from the ground. She asked, "Are you okay?" When she reached out to assist him, Will rejected her help, brushing her hand away. He palmed his knee as he eventually rose from the ground.

"Leave me alone," he demanded. He then placed his hands into the pockets of the hoodie he was wearing and walked away from the girl with tears in his eyes.

Thunder roared as a flash of lightning consumed the sky. The rain pour became heavier, further obstructing the view from Will's window, and more importantly, the view of the front window.

"Watch the road!" the girl in the front passenger side yelled.

"Chill," the driver responded. "I got this."

Will turned his head away from the window and finally noticed his free hand under the hand of the girl sitting across from him. When she noticed that Will was no longer looking at the window, she began to smile at him. Another flash of lightning filled the sky with another roar of thunder.

Eleven-year-old Will sat on the swing, looking down at the dirt on the ground underneath his feet as he gripped the chains that connected the swing to the set. Other children stood around each other in the distance. Will could barely see them, not that he was trying hard to do so, but he could hear their voices loud and clear.

"Why do you hang out with him? He's weird."

"Yeah, he never says anything."

"Plus, he sucks at basketball."

"All he does is read those books. What a scrub."

"Hey, wait! Where you going? Man, she's as hopeless as he is. C'mon, y'all, let's go somewhere else."

The group dispersed. However, one girl from the group walked in Will's direction, and eventually joined him, sitting on the swing next to him. She noticed him looking down at the ground and smiled at him.

Without looking up, Will asked the girl, "Why don't you listen to them? Why do you keep hanging around me?"

She answered, "Because I'm your friend! Or at least I'd like to be."

"But why? Why would you want to be friends with someone like me?"

"Because you shouldn't have to be alone, Will! Don't you get that?!"

Will didn't respond to her at first. He tilted his head back up and gripped the chains even harder. Without looking at her, he finally said, "Well, what if I want to be alone? Have you ever considered that, April?"

"Yes, I have. And I don't think that's true," April answered. "I think you want someone you can just…talk to. You look like you have a lot to say, and you don't have anyone to say it to. You read all those books. Don't you want to talk about them with somebody? Or when you're sad or angry, don't you wish there was someone you could talk to about it? When you sit there on that swing, wouldn't it be nice if there was someone sitting beside you? Not even swinging. Just talking."

Will closed his eyes, hoping that it would conceal the water that was coming from them. "Yes," he answered with a sullen tone.

"Well then, let me be that for you!" April pleaded. "I want to be someone you can talk to about anything! Can I?"

Will finally looked at April and answered, "Okay."

"How many did you have?!" the girl in the front passenger seat asked the driver.

"I only had like two or three! Man, stop trippin'!" he answered. Taking his eyes off the road, he attempted to look back at Will and April.

"Will. April. Y'all good back there?" he asked.

April nodded her head nervously, and Will didn't respond at all.

"Pay attention to the damn road!" the girl in front shouted. The rain became even heavier, so much that the windshield wipers weren't able to keep up. The girl said, "Look, just pull over to the side, and let me drive."

"Hey, just shut up!" the boy shouted at the girl. When he saw the girl's reaction, he calmly added, "Look, let's just get those two back home so we can get back to the party! It's bad enough we were late picking them up."

Suddenly, there was yet another clash of thunder and strike of lightning.

"OW!" thirteen-year-old Will shouted before covering his black left eye. April retreated from him, holding the still dampened towel she had attempted to apply to the affected eye. "I'll be fine," he assured her as he attempted to stand back up. It was hard for him to do so at first, but he managed to press his bruised hand against the grey lockers he was sitting by for leverage. He then took that bruised hand and wiped the blood that had run down to his blue hoodie from his lip.

"What happened?" April asked Will.

"I slipped and fell down some stairs," Will answered sarcastically.

"But the school doesn't have stairs. You know, sarcasm doesn't suit you well, Will."

"Yeah. I also know that you, along with my parents, wouldn't stop harping on about the importance of good grades and how I had so much 'potential.' So I study, and I study, and somehow I get all A's this term."

Will pointed directly at his bruised eye and continued, "And this is my reward for doing so."

"Will, I didn't think that…"

"It's not your fault, April. This black eye isn't punishment, it's…ch…Salem's way of bringing me back to reality. And speaking of reality…"

The two were joined by a large black woman wearing a smoke grey two-button jacket with matching trousers. She was holding a megaphone in her left hand that she used to direct traffic in the halls.

"Hello, Mrs. Pickett," Will greeted continuing his earlier speech.

"Fighting again, Moon? You are aware of our zero tolerance policy, right?" she asked.

"I am. And where were you to enforce that policy when the fighting was actually happening?" Will asked.

"I'm only one person, Moon. I can't be all over this campus at once. Let's go to the office. We'll call your parents and have them pick you up," Pickett replied.

April pleaded, "But it wasn't his fault, Mrs. Pickett. Will…"

"Is going to be suspended for three days as per our rules and regulations, Ms. Foster. Now if you don't want to share his fate,

I'd advise you to stay out of this. Furthermore, I would highly suggest you stay away from troublemakers like Mr. Moon here in the future," Pickett interrupted. She then grabbed Will by the bruised arm and led him away.

Suddenly, Will heard the loud blare of the horn coming from a car on the other side of the road. The driver of the car Will was in quickly swerved to the right, barely preventing a collision. Both Will and April in the backseat gasped in fear as the driver pulled off the feat.

"Did you not see that car coming?!" the girl in the front passenger seat asked in a confrontational tone.

"Yeah, I saw it! Why did you think I turned?! Will you just chill out already?! I can't concentrate on the road with you all up in my ear!" the driver said.

"Then pull over and let me drive!"

"Why?! You think I'm drunk, don't you?! You drank as many as I did! Just shut up! Everybody just shut up!" His tone was louder than the thunder that, once again, filled the skies. Along with the thunder came more lightning.

Fourteen-year-old Will covered his eyes for a second. He was blinded by the flash of the Polaroid camera being operated by his mother.

Liz pulled out the photo from the camera, shook it for a few seconds, took a quick look at it, and said, "Nope, this one isn't good. Okay, you two, let's get another one. Oooh! I know! Why don't you two go stand by the porch?"

April grabbed Will by the hand and took him to the front of the porch of his house. She re-wrapped her arms around his and cheerfully said to Liz, "Okay, Mrs. Liz, we're ready!"

"Okay, you two," Liz said. "Smile real big!"

The two complied. April's smile was genuine whereas Will's seemed forced. He hadn't smiled much in his lifetime, so for him, this was a very difficult task. "Three…two…one," Liz counted down as she took the picture. When the picture was ready, she pulled it out of the camera, shook it, and took a look at it. She was amazed at how well it came out. "Oh…my…goodness, you two are so adorable!" she said gleefully.

"Anthony! Come see this!" Liz called out to the driveway of the house. Anthony exited the driver's seat of the Isuzu Rodeo and walked towards the porch to take a look at the photo. Reacting to the photo, Anthony complimented, "Well, y'all two look good for your little date."

"It's not a date, Dad," Will said with a blushed face. "We… we're just going to the movies," he continued nervously.

"What movie are you guys going to see again?" Liz asked.

"*The Phantom Menace*. The local theater just got it in," Will answered.

"That *Star Wars* stuff is for little boys," April said. Then she tightened her grip around Will and added, "But it is his birthday after all. Oh, and don't worry, Mr. and Mrs. Moon. My brother will pick us up from the movies and take us back home."

"Okay. The car's running, so you two hop in."

Will and April entered the back passenger seats of the vehicle. Liz waved at the two, and April enthusiastically waved back.

"What are you doing?! Are you crazy?! Let go of the damn wheel!" April's brother shouted at the girl beside him.

"No! We shouldn't be driving right now! Just pull over and let this rain die down!" The girl wouldn't let go of the wheel. She frantically continued to turn it to the right, hoping she could steer the car to the emergency stop lane. April's brother shoved her against the window and regained full control of the steering wheel.

Unfortunately, he wasn't able to regain control in time. While April's brother was struggling with the girl in the front seat, the still-moving car ended up on the other side of the road. He wasn't able to swerve back to the right side of the road in time as he had done before. The only thing Will and the others could see was the bright flash of the lights of the large tractor-trailer coming right toward them. The only thing Will could hear was the very loud honk coming from the rig followed by April's brother's scream of "OH SHHH—!"

A bright white light enveloped the entire area. Nothing else could be seen, but a constant beeping noise could be heard. Soon, the white light faded, revealing a hospital room. Lying in the bed, Will regained consciousness and looked around, slowly realizing where he was. However, he wasn't dressed as if he had spent a considerable amount of time in a hospital. He was instead wearing a grey hoodie along with a pair of blue jeans. He detached the wires that connected his arm to the monitor and climbed out of the bed. He was fully aware of where he was, how he had gotten there, and what would come next.

He didn't run to the nurses' station this time. Instead, he walked towards the elevator near it. He noticed that none of the plaques next to the doors of the other rooms on the floor had names on them this time. Additionally, as he approached the elevator, he noticed that there was nobody occupying the nurses' station: no doctors to sedate him, no security officers to pursue him.

Will pressed the call button, and the elevator doors opened immediately. He entered the elevator, and when he pressed the button correlating to the floor he wanted to go to, the doors instantly closed and the elevator started going down. He only wanted to go down two floors, but it seemed that the elevator was taking a very long time to do so. As Will stood in the elevator waiting to arrive at his destination, he began to hear several faint voices coming from an unknown location.

"What's past is past," said the first voice.

"You'll get by with a little help from your friends," said a second voice.

"Those who fail to learn from history… Well, you know the rest," said the last voice.

A chime came from the elevator as its doors opened. Will exited the elevator. Right across from him was the room he wanted to enter. Again, there was no name on the plaque next to the door. Furthermore, it was the only room on this floor. Will looked to both the left and right of the room and saw nothing but white on both ends. He turned around and was shocked to see that the elevator was gone, completely replaced by the same whiteness that consumed the rest of the floor.

With no other choice, Will entered the room. It looked just like the room he had been in earlier, but there were two beds placed parallel to each other and surrounded by curtains. There was a chair in between the beds placed against the wall on the far end of the room. Sitting in that chair was the eleven-year-old Will, wearing the same hoodie he always wore on the swings.

"Y'know, at first I thought she was our friend because she felt sorry for us. She pitied us for being so weak and pathetic. To her, we were nothing more than a charity case, someone she could say she helped so she'd feel good about herself.

"But then, only too late did it dawn on me. That wasn't the case. No, she was our friend because we had one very specific thing in common with each other. We're both stubborn as hell. We spent years asking her to leave us alone, pushing her away from us so that we could be to ourselves. But she wouldn't give up, would she?

"No, we pushed, and she only pushed harder, and eventually, she got her way. We became her friend, and for a time we fooled ourselves into thinking we were happy. But you and I both know there's only one way a relationship with us can end.

"But she was stubborn, just as you are. I thought I was able to make it clear to you that we are meant to be alone. That absolute alienation is our fate." The younger Will hopped from his chair and walked towards Will, stopping right between the two hospital beds. "But you won't listen. You want others to suffer as she did. Oh? Did you think that it's going to be different this time? Did you think that just because you're living a 'new life' that you're a 'new you?' You did, didn't you?!"

The younger Will pointed at Will and laughed hysterically, falling to the floor with force. This was the first time either Will had laughed, and he was certainly enjoying it. But, eventually, he stopped laughing. Still on his knees, he looked down at the floor and said to Will, "You can run as fast and as far as you want to, but no matter what, you cannot escape fate. And you certainly can't change it."

After saying that, the younger Will simply vanished. Afterward, the curtains surrounding the two beds were opened automatically, fully revealing the beds. Then, the sheets that had completely covered the bodies occupying the beds slowly became undone, revealing the identity of the bodies.

Will's eyes opened very wide as he stood in complete shock and horror at the revelation. He was completely unable to move an inch of his body after seeing who occupied the two beds. In one bed was a fully unconscious Nathan. In the other, Ashley lay in the same state.

Will continued to gasp for air. As seconds passed, he found it harder and harder to breathe. It was as if he was being choked by the very air he gasped for. Though they were heavy, his breaths could not drown out the beep of the flatlining coming from the heart monitors Nathan and Ashley were hooked up to. The sound of the flatlines grew louder and louder as the white light that surrounded the room started consuming everything around Will.

Chapter Twelve

Thursday, August 26, 1999

Will lay diagonally across his bed with both his arms and legs stretched out. He was drowning in a small puddle of his own sweat, despite the ceiling fan rotating on full blast. His eyes, which looked up at the ceiling, were wide open exposing the blood red veins in the sclerae. It had been hours since he had last closed them or even blinked. The alarm clock on the dresser next to his bed read 8:02 a.m. He had been in this exact state for the past five hours.

There didn't seem to be anything that could move Will from the bed, not even the desire to silence the voices of the annoying radio personalities that came from his alarm clock.

"You're listening to Wake and Bake with Skizzle and Captain Crunch only here on The Heat 98.5, blazin' Ingram Park with the hottest Hip-Hop and R&B. What it is, y'all? It's your boy Captain Crunch."

"And y'all already know it's Skizzle from the South Side!"

"Okay, Skizz, we're about to take some calls from the listeners. Caller, you're on the air with Skizzle and The Captain. What's up?"

"Hey, Skizz and Captain, I just wanted to call and tell you guys that you're full of crap!"

"Oh word, caller?"

"Yeah, man! It isn't Y2K or robots that are gonna kill us in the end. It's aliens, man! They've been living among us for billions of years underground, just waiting for the right time to rise up and destroy us all! And this is the year it all happens, man! This is their time, man! The future can't change! It refuses to, man!"

"Yeah, whatever, man. Next caller, you're on with Skizz and Captain Crunch. What's up?"

"Heeeey! This is Tamika from Riverside. I got a question for Skizzle."

"What's good, ma?"

"Can you tell me what 6,114 times twelve is?"

"Not off the top of my head, baby girl. Tell me what is it?"

"It's the amount of back child support you owe me, you no good son of a—!"

"Next caller!"

The radio show hosts continued to take questions from callers until the commercial break interrupted them. However, Will didn't hear any of it playing in the background, nor did he hear the heavy knocks at his bedroom door. The door busted open, and Liz entered the room.

"WILLIAM!" Liz finally called out to him. "Why are you still in bed?! Do you have any idea what time it is?!"

Will slowly turned his head to the clock on the dresser and came to the realization that he was far past late for school. His reaction wasn't one of shock or surprise, however. He turned off the alarm and slowly rose from his bed. He sat on the edge of the bed facing his mother as she continued her interrogation.

"Are those the same clothes you wore yesterday? What did I tell you about sleeping in your clothes?"

Will rubbed his eyes, and then completely got up from the bed. Without a word, he grabbed some clothes, including another hoodie, from the pile of folded clothes from the larger dresser. Finally, he walked passed his mother as he exited the bedroom and headed to the bathroom.

Once again, Will went through the motions of his morning hygiene routine. Twenty-five minutes later, he was heading downstairs, fully dressed with backpack in hand. Liz was in the kitchen preparing to leave the house for work.

"I can't drop you off at school and make it to work at time," she told Will.

"It's fine, I'll walk. Should only take me twenty minutes or so," he responded in a dull tone.

"Well, since you're already late, you might as well get some breakfast."

"I'm not hungry."

"I'm not asking, William. Grab something to eat now!"

"Yes, ma'am," Will said in a miffed tone. He headed to the pantry inside the kitchen. To his luck, he was able to find a box with one package of strawberry Pop-Tarts inside the pantry, meaning he wouldn't have to resort to the granola bars or sugar-free, fiber rich cereals that Liz kept in abundance. He immediately unwrapped the package and began eating the Pop-Tarts. Liz headed towards the front door while Will stayed in the kitchen and ate the Pop-Tarts. A few minutes later, Will finished his breakfast, grabbed his backpack from the kitchen floor, and left the house behind his mother.

Outside, Will walked towards the sidewalk leading to the main street. As he passed the driveway, Liz, sitting in her car still in the driveway, waved goodbye to him. Will disingenuously waved back. A few minutes into his walk to school, Will paused to put on his earbuds and turn on his CD player. However, as he grabbed the right earbud, he sighed and put it back into the pockets of his hoodie.

The sounds of the songs Will would've normally listened to were replaced by the loud morning traffic. He found the crossing over to Benbrook Street nearly impossible at this time of day. Cars heading to work flooded the intersecting road. Even when the light on that side of the road was green, the traffic showed no sign of moving. With no other choice, Will stood on the corner of the street and waited for the traffic to die down. This took about twenty minutes.

When Will was finally able to cross over to Benbrook Street, he found his walk to be more peaceful. But Will himself was not in a peaceful mood. His movement and overall demeanor were evidence of the lack of sleep he had gotten the night before and the nightmares that caused it that still weighed heavily on his mind. As he continued his walk down the street, he was eventually joined, once again, by the girl in the white dress.

"Go away, I'm not in the mood," Will demanded of her.

She didn't say anything to Will, she continued to walk beside him. Will became irritated by this and, in time, asked, "What do you want from me?!"

Again, she didn't answer; she continued to walk right by his side with a look of concern for him. "ARRGH! FINE! Just walk, then!" Will shouted with his fists clenched. He placed his arms back into his pockets, and the two continued their walk.

Fifteen or so minutes later, Will found himself in front of the Washington High campus, facing the statue of George Washington once again. Rather than look at the statue, he looked to his left to see if the girl was still beside him. She wasn't; he didn't know at what point she had disappeared again. The campus exterior was almost empty as the bell for first period had already rung. Will walked across the campus to the D building, where his class for this period was located. He didn't want to be stopped by any of the patrolling security officers, so he ducked into the adjoining C building as soon as he could.

Will finally made it to his first period class. He was about twenty minutes late, something the biology teacher, Mrs. Caldwell, wasn't too happy about.

"Don't sit down just yet, Mr. Moon," she said to him while he was still near the door. "Since you like to interrupt my lecture with your tardiness, then it's safe to assume that you can tell the class in which step of cell division does crossing over occur?"

Will certainly was in no mood for this. He answered, "No, I can't. I couldn't answer that even if I were here on time.

Fortunately, there's someone in this room right now whose very job is to do just that."

Mrs. Caldwell pulled out a white referral form from her desk and started filling it out.

"You are correct, Mr. Moon, it is my job to teach that. It's also my job to discipline any student who prevents me from doing so. So don't bother taking your seat. It's obvious from your tardiness and attitude that you don't want to be here." She handed the referral to Will and continued, "So you can just march right to Terrell's office instead."

Will exited the class without complaint. He wanted to slam the door behind him, but he was able to resist the urge to do so. He doubled back towards the administration building. As Will walked down the hall of the C building, he could hear the sound of someone panting. He kept walking, and the panting sound grew heavier. Halfway down the hallway, the person from whom the panting came crashed into Will and fell to the ground. It was revealed to be Rob lying on the floor. His panting had turned into wheezing. Will didn't help him back up on his feet. He wanted to just keep walking to the vice-principal's office, but Rob called out to him.

"Hold up, homie," Rob said breathing heavily.

"What?" Will asked still looking forward.

Rob grabbed his left knee and lifted himself up. "Just wait a second," he said still panting.

"I don't have time for this."

"Okay, homie. J-just hold up for a few seconds. Then you can bounce."

"Fine."

Will reluctantly honored Rob's request and remained where he was. Rob wiped the sweat from his face and breathed a sigh of relief.

Then, he looked over Will's shoulder and loudly said, "Yeah, what's up now, chumps?! Let's see how hard y'all are now that I got my homie here with me! I done warned y'all about tryin' to run up on The Rob Squad! And now all three of you bustas is 'bout to get got!"

Will instantly knew Rob wasn't addressing him. He turned around to see the same three boys who were harassing Rob by the lockers two days ago. The three approached Will and Rob in a threatening demeanor.

Rob stood a few paces behind Will as they were confronted by the three boys. With his hands in his pockets and without saying anything, Will stared at the boys with the same look as before. This time was different, however; no one miraculously showed up out of nowhere to break up this confrontation. Will was still irritated from earlier, and it showed in his facial expression. What didn't show was the fear Will was feeling. The boys didn't know this, but Will's track record when it came to fights was not impressive in the least. On top of that, Will believed that if and when this situation came to blows, Rob wouldn't be backing him up in a physical fashion. Will's only option at this point was to bide his time and hope that something or someone would intervene like last time.

One of the boys started to lunge forward as if they were ready to start the fight, causing Rob to flinch a little. But he was interrupted by the boy in the middle of the formation, who extended his arms out to his sides to stop the two boys beside him.

"You know what?" he asked Rob and Will. "We're not doing this today. But don't worry, you two are gonna get what's coming to you, and you're gonna get it real soon." The boy then pointed at Will and said, "Especially you." The three walked past Will and Rob. One of them incidentally bumped into Will's shoulder on his way.

After the boys were out of hearing distance, Rob turned towards them and claimed yet another victory. "The only thing we gettin' is all up in yo' girlfriends, you pasty faced bustas! Rob Squad in the building! What, son? What?!" Rob continued to boast with accompanying barking noises.

Will, on the other hand, was far from as happy as Rob that the confrontation was over. He took his hands from out his pockets and clenched his fists. His patience with Rob had completely run out. Will turned to Rob, who was still bragging to himself. Then, with as much strength as he could muster up, he shoved Rob in the back, forcing him to fall to the ground.

"Damn, homie! What's your beef?" Rob asked confused as to what had just happened.

Will pointed at Rob and said, "Get this through your thick skull. You and I are not homies!" His tone was angry, but not loud so as to alert any figures of authority that may be patrolling nearby.

"What you mean, you and me ain't homies? Man, we all we got in the struggle!"

"Do you even listen to the words that come from your mouth?! Do you have any idea as to what it is you're talking about?! What do you know about any struggle?! If you went through even half of what I have, seen what I've seen, you damn sure wouldn't be sitting here pretending that any of it would be something to glorify!"

Rob didn't say a word.

"Let me tell you something about the so-called 'hood' life you're emulating. There isn't a damn thing pretty about it. Whatever music videos you've been watching to learn how to copy that lifestyle don't even begin to paint a picture of how much it sucks! So believe me when I tell you that I don't need to be hanging around someone that constantly reminds me of it, even if he's doing a crappy job at it. So just stay the hell away from me, Robert!" Will placed his hands back into his pockets and resumed his walk towards the administration building.

Rob's only response to Will's rant was, "It's Rob, man. None of that Robert stuff."

Will finally made it across campus to the administration building. He came across a woman standing against the wall next to the door leading to the main office with her arms folded. She stood about six-foot-tall and had a pale brown skin complexion; it seemed that she was of Asian heritage. The woman had a long, black ponytail that went down past her shoulders. She was wearing an expensive-looking combination of a red jacket and black skirt with matching black heels. Around her neck was a lanyard that looked similar to the one that Will's dad normally wore. When Will walked past her to get to the door to the office, she gave him the most intimidating stare he had ever come across. On any other occasion, he would have been scared stiff of the woman, but today, anger was Will's primary emotion regarding everything.

Inside the office, Will took the same chair he had sat in on Tuesday. Across from him, two men stood over the secretary's desk. They were both wearing full suits, one in a medium blue, the other in black. The man in the blue suit was much older than the other, as evident from his completely grey hair and wrinkles across his face. The man in the black suit looked to be in his late thirties to early forties. He had coiffed brown hair. He also had well-trimmed facial hair which included a goatee, mustache, and sideburns that connected them to his hair. He was also wearing a lanyard around his neck, similar to the one worn by the woman outside.

"I believe that Washington will be the perfect school for her," said the man in the black suit.

"And we will do everything in our power to accommodate her," the man in the blue suit replied. His voice sounded familiar to Will. It was one he had heard multiple times before.

"I do not doubt that you will. She will be here next Monday."

"We'll have everything ready for her by then. I'll have Claudia here process her information and get her into the system ASAP."

"Thanks for admitting her on such a short notice."

"Oh, don't worry about it. It's not a problem at all."

The two men shook hands. The man in the blue suit retreated to an office with the word "Phillip Caine - Principal" on the door. The man in the black suit exited the office and joined the woman standing outside. The two left the administration building together.

With no one between him and the secretary, Will got up from his chair, walked to the secretary's desk, and handed her the referral. The secretary got up from her chair and walked to the vice-principal's office. She knocked on his door and entered. Meanwhile, Will sat back down in his chair. Two minutes passed and the secretary came back outside from Terrell's office. Before returning to her desk, she looked at Will and said to him, "He'll see you now."

Will entered Vice-Principal Terrell's office and took one of the two chairs next to his desk. Terrell sat at his desk reading the referral that was given to him by the secretary. He then placed it down on his desk and started to address Will.

"Showing up twenty minutes late for class and immediately back-talking the teacher? I thought I put you on the right path, Moon. I give you some amnesty and placed you in a position where you can start to build some self-esteem and do some good. And here you are, yet again sitting in my office with that same angry look on your face, getting into even more trouble. I do all of that for you and I get nothing in return. Do you have any idea how foolish that makes me look? Do you know how much that hurts my heart? Do you even have anything to say for yourself?"

"No, sir," Will answered.

"I didn't think so." Terrell entered a few keystrokes on his computer. "I also don't think it would be good for you to remain in school today. So I'll be calling your parents and having them pick you up. You are to sit outside until they arrive. Do you understand?"

"Yes, sir," Will answered.

"Then go," Terrell said.

Will rose from the chair and exited Terrell's office. He sat back down in the chair in the waiting area. He sat there for an hour before someone arrived to pick him up from school. To his discontent, it was his dad who entered the office. He was in the business casual wear he reserved for work, complete with his lanyard. Will's concern wasn't with his dad's clothing, which implied that he had skipped out on work to be here. It was the angry look on his father's face that he was focused on. He hadn't seen that look on Anthony in a very long time.

Chapter Thirteen

THE RIDE HOME WAS FILLED with silence. This came as a surprise to Will as he was certain that his father would be yelling at him for the entire trip. The trip was also longer than it should have been. The midday traffic was already starting to build up, adding to Anthony's frustration. Will tried his hardest to avoid looking at his father. He couldn't help but make a few quick glances at him, however. In those brief glances, he noticed that Anthony's scowl had not changed whatsoever since the two left the office at school.

For the majority of the ride home, Will looked out of the window on his side of the car. Though neither of the two said anything, and the radio was completely off, Will could once again hear voices ring in his head.

"Boy, we are so tired of having to take time out of work to come to your school. What is it with behaving that's hard for you to comprehend?"

Ten-year-old William sat in a wooden chair inside the office of the principal of Reynolds Elementary School. To his left sat his mother with her arms folded as she impatiently tapped her left foot against the floor. She was dressed in a maroon polo with the logo of the fast food restaurant she worked at part-time on the left side of her chest and a badge with her name on it pinned on the right. To complement the work polo, she was wearing pitch black slacks and black shoes that looked uncomfortable for anyone to wear. Her purse leaned against the leg of her chair on the floor; the visor she was required to wear at work was sticking out of it. To his right sat his father, as angry as ever. He, too, donned his work apparel, a blue button-up shirt with khaki pants. Like with his mother, his father's badge for work was pinned to his chest, although it was a bit bigger and contained more information on it.

Will didn't answer his father's question. His head was down in the chair as he looked towards the floor. He tried as best as he could to hide the mixed emotion of fear and anger on his face.

"Did you not hear your father ask you a question?" Liz asked Will.

"Yes, ma'am," Will answered quietly, still looking to the ground.

"Well then, answer him! And hold your head up!" Liz demanded.

Will started to open his mouth to answer Anthony's question, but he knew there wasn't an answer that would satisfy him. Even if, in this particular case, Will wasn't in the wrong. The very fact that his parents were called in and were sitting in the office with him was proof of guilt enough. Will didn't have long to think of an excuse, legitimate or otherwise, regardless. The door to the office opened, and the principal, Victoria Chambers, entered the room, taking her seat across from the Moon family.

The most interesting thing to note of Principal Chambers were her eyes. She wore some pretty thick glasses, but they couldn't conceal the wrinkles around her eyes brought on by countless years of stress. The looks of stress were dominant in that region, but her entire mocha-tinted face showed signs of years of stress in some way shape or form. The signs led all the way up to her unkempt hair which contained streaks of silver, more than most people for someone in her late thirties.

After taking her seat, Principal Chambers pushed aside the stack of folders and forms that sat on her desk and completely obstructed her view of the Moon family. Folders and forms were the majority of the things that her office was comprised of, save for the shoddy furniture. With the exception of her university degree, there were no awards or accolades filling the walls of her office. In fact, the only other thing hanging from her wall was a framed newspaper clipping. It featured a picture of a seven-year-old Victoria with other kids being escorted by several police officials. The headline read, "Black Youth Take First Steps into Newly Integrated School." Underneath the headline read, "Protesting white families begin leaving Salem en masse," in smaller type.

It took Principal Chambers a few minutes to shuffle the things on her desk around so that she was able to see the Moon Family. Afterwards, she interlocked her fingers and began to address the parents.

"Thank you for taking time out to come to the school today, Mr. and Mrs. Moon," she began.

"Uh-huh. What's this all about? What he do this time?" Anthony interrupted.

"William got into an altercation with some other boys in his class. It became very loud and disruptive, so his teacher sent him to me. According to his teacher, this is the third time it's happened this week."

"Why were you being loud in class?" Liz asked Will.

"They kept picking on me!" Will answered loudly.

"That's not an excuse!" Anthony responded almost as loud. "What have your mama and me said that you should do when the other kids pick on you? Didn't we tell you to ignore them?"

"I did! I got as far away as I could from them. All I wanted to do was read my book, but they kept coming to me and picking on me! Why won't just leave me alone?!" Will's tone of voice became louder with each word.

"Hush, boy! Stop being all dramatic," Anthony demanded.

"Mr. and Mrs. Moon, William's teacher has told me that he doesn't talk or play with the other kids in his class. Forgive my bluntness, but I've been a principal at this school for many years and I've noticed that the more outgoing and social kids tend to gang up on the quiet, introverted ones. This is because they see them as easy targets, and let's face it, they usually are."

"So what you're saying is if Will made some friends, he wouldn't be picked on as much?" Liz asked the principal.

"Maybe, Mrs. Moon."

"So why don't you make some friends then, boy?" Anthony asked.

"Because they all hate me," Will answered.

"That can't be true," Liz said.

"It is! They all call me names. They say I'm weird because all I do is read books! They don't wanna be my friend. And that's fine because I don't wanna be theirs. I just want everyone to leave me alone! Just let me be by myself!" Will's voice raised again.

"Boy, I ain't gonna tell you to lower your voice again!"

"What if he doesn't want to or can't make friends?" Liz inquired. "What can we do to stop this from constantly happening? Principal Chambers, we can't keep coming up to the school for this. Anthony and I both work full-time jobs and go to school on the side. Plus we have a two-year-old daughter to take care of."

Without immediately answering, Principal Chambers got up from her chair and walked to the half opened door. She poked her head out for a second and brought it back inside. She then closed the door and locked it from the inside. Anthony, Liz and Will looked in confusion as she did this; they didn't take their eyes off of her once until after she sat back down in her chair.

"I am going to be brutally honest here, Mr. and Mrs. Moon. I look at William, and to an extent his younger brother, and I see something I don't see too much in other students here. I see potential, a desire and ability to succeed. Let's be honest here. Most of these kids in this school? You and I both know that they're going to do time in juvenile hall and have probation officers before they leave eighth grade, if they even make it that far. They're not going to amount to much; they'll go down the same path as the people in their lives did. I know this because I've seen it happen too many times before.

But not your children. I actually see bright futures for them. I see that in them, because I see that in you two. I only called one of you here, and yet both of you arrived, very quickly might I add, and taking time out of your busy schedules to do so. And that, Mr. and Mrs. Moon, speaks volumes.

So let me offer so my solution to this problem. Don't let them get to you, William. Look, I can bring those other kids in here and yell at them until I'm blue in the face. I can give them detention and even suspend them. But it won't change a thing. They know where their actions will take them and they choose to take that road regardless. That's the reality of this town. There isn't anything for a lot of people here outside of drug dealing and gangbanging, and they know that. But then they look at someone like you and they don't see someone willing to go down that same path. So they will try to drag you down with them, kicking and screaming if need be. Don't let them."

The members of the Moon Family got up from their chairs and exited the office. They made their way towards the front entrance of the school. On the way Will came across April walking in the hall holding a couple of textbooks. The two looked at each other as they passed each other by. April would give Will a very warm smile as she walked by.

"Get out of the car, boy!"

Anthony's command brought Will back to reality. He did as he was told, exiting the vehicle and walking towards the front door of the house behind Anthony. Anthony would continue to bark orders at Will, "Go straight to your room. Don't turn on no TV. Don't listen to any music. Don't do nothin'. Don't even breathe heavy. Just sit there. Imma fix me a sandwich, catch the midday numbers, and then I'll be up there to deal with you."

Once again, Will complied, heading straight to his room and closing the door behind him. Will placed his backpack in the far right corner of his room and then sat on his bed. He placed his arms back in his pockets and looked down at the ground yet again. Without shifting his focus whatsoever, Will said, "I thought I said I wasn't in the mood for this today."

Will was addressing April, once again wearing the white dress, who was now sitting beside him on the bed. And once again, she did not respond. Additionally, her look of concern for him returned. Will asked the girl again, "What do you want?!" His tone was silent as to not gain the attention of his father downstairs. April proceeded to place her arm around Will and leaned in a little to place her head on his shoulder. Will lifted his head up and noticed her gesture even if he couldn't physically feel it.

She answered him, "I want to talk. Like we used to all the time."

"I don't have anything to say," Will responded.

"Yes you do," she rebutted. "You have a lot to say."

"Well, I don't want to talk about it."

"Yes, you do. You've held it in for so long. And you want to let it all out. But for some reason you're holding back. Why is that?"

Will hopped up from his bed and answered, "What am I supposed to say, huh? Do you want me to confess to you?! Is that why you're here?! Is that why you won't go away?! I could beg you for forgiveness until the day I die! And I probably will! But none it would bring you back! None of it could change what I did to you!"

"I don't understand. What do you do to me?"

"What do you mean you don't…I killed you!" Will was almost certain his father heard that. But he didn't care.

"You…killed…me?" April asked. "No, that can't be right." She rose from the bed and stood beside him. "I was in a car crash. I mean, you were there. But you were in the backseat next to me. You weren't the one driving."

Will grew angrier, but the anger wasn't necessarily directed at the girl. "But we wouldn't have even been in that car if you would've just listened to me! If you would have just…"

"Left you alone?!" she interrupted raising her voice for the very first time. "Is that what you wanted to say?"

"YES!" Will shouted even louder. "If you would've just listened to those other kids… If you would've ignored me like the nobody I was…like the nobody I am…you'd still be alive right now! Why don't you get that?! Why doesn't anybody get that?! What in the hell is it about me that everybody finds so interesting that they absolutely have to involve me in their lives?!"

The girl clenched her fists, and in a loud outburst, she responded, "You aren't a nobody! Why don't YOU get that?! You're special! You have the potential to do great things, and everybody you have ever come across saw that, whether they liked it or not!

"That's why I couldn't 'just leave you alone!' Because I saw that in you, more than anybody, and I wanted to do everything in my power to get you to see that! But you never will! Not as long as you try so hard to push everyone away! Not as long as you hide yourself from the world! You have this amazing life, and I know that you are going to do great things in it! But you have to live it, William! You promised me that you would!"

Will was taken back by this revelation. The girl's words pierced through his chest and right to his heart. Tears began to roll down his eyes. They were slow at first, but suddenly they rushed down his face like a torrent of water falling down a cliff. The words he formed in response were broken, and he struggled to convey them, "B-but it's not f-fair. I w-wanted you t-to be here. You d-deserve to be here…to…l-live this life with me."

April moved closer to Will and hugged him. Will couldn't feel it physically, but he was affected by the hug regardless.

The girl said to him, "But I am here with you, Will. And I always will be."

A few moments later, Will used his hands to wipe the tears that had now blurred his vision. When he could finally see again, it was not the girl that stood in front of him. Instead, it was his father. Will didn't know how much of his conversation with the girl his dad was there for, but he didn't care either.

"It wasn't your fault, William," Anthony assured him.

"I-I think I know that now, Dad," Will responded still wiping the tears from his eyes.

"So that's what this was all about?" Anthony let out a sigh. He then placed the leather belt he had in his hand on Will's dresser. "Sit down, boy," he commanded. Will obeyed and sat back down on the bed.

"Look, I know how tough it is to lose someone you care about, especially at a young age. And I know it's been especially tough on you. After all, she was your only friend at the time, right?"

"Yes, sir."

"We didn't necessarily give you enough time to say goodbye to the girl. Shoot, we didn't even get to go to the funeral. We kinda just up and left as soon as I got that phone call from TaylorCorp. We were so busy with buying the house and moving in and getting you kids situated that we didn't even stop to think about how you were dealing with someone you just lost.

"Your mama and me saw you walking around like you always do, with your hands in your pockets like you didn't have a care in the world. We would've never guessed that this whole time, you were blaming yourself for her death. And the guilt was eating at you. You were holding it all in until you couldn't anymore, weren't you?"

"Yes, sir."

"Don't do that, boy! Don't hold nothin' in like that! If something like that's on your mind, talk to somebody about it! You're a teenager now, and y'all don't really like talking to your parents. And I remember all those counselors we tried getting you to talk to. But you would just sit in those offices refusing to speak to total strangers. But maybe your mama's right. Maybe you should get you some friends, some real good ones that you can talk to about stuff like this."

After hearing his dad's speech, Will's now dried eyes lit up. "You know, I think I already do," he said enthusiastically. Well, as enthusiastically as he could, anyway.

"Well, that's good." Anthony replied. "Now then, I ain't gonna be gettin' any more calls from the school telling me to come get you, am I?"

"No, sir," Will answered.

"Okay. Well then, I tell you what. Imma let this one slide. I ain't even gonna tell ya mama. If she comes home early and asks why you're here, you tell her…I don't know…they had to spray the school down or somethin', make somethin' up."

"Yes, sir."

"But you know my motto, boy."

"Do it right the first time?"

"No, the other one."

"Stay out of my M&M's?"

"No, the other other one!"

"Nothing in this world comes free?"

"Yeah, that one. So in return, when your mama asks, and you know she will, you gonna tell her that it was you that accidentally taped over her show today. Deal?"

Will looked up at his father from his bed and answered, "Deal."

"Okay, good. Now, come on downstairs and make yourself a sandwich for lunch."

"Yes, sir," Will responded.

Chapter Fourteen

Will and Anthony sat in the living room to eat the sandwiches they had prepared for themselves minutes earlier. While Will sat on the couch, Anthony sat in the recliner adjacent to it. He was the only person allowed to do so. As the two ate, they watched the television across from them. Every now and then, Will would glance over at his dad to see the disgusted looks on his face in reaction to what was on TV. He found it hilarious, but he didn't laugh.

"Jenny, my mom needs to stop trippin' and stay out of my life! I'm fifteen years old, and that means I'm a grown ass woman! I can do what I want when I want! If I wanna stay out all night, I'm gonna! If I wanna smoke and drink, I'm gonna do that, too! And if I wanna beat someone down for hatin' on me, Imma do that! I do what I want!"

The young girl on the TV's speech was met with thunderous jeers from the studio audience. She replied to them with, "Sit down! Shut up! Y'all don't know me! Y'all just hatin' 'cuz y'all can't be like me! Whateva! Whateva!"

Will looked at his dad again. His mouth was ajar with awe in regard to what he was watching. Anthony finally noticed that Will was looking at him and asked, "How can y'all watch this stuff?"

"Guilty pleasure," Will answered. "You can change the channel. The remote's right there on the arm of your chair."

"Don't wanna. I done already taped over your mama's show once. I'm not touching this thing again."

"Well, if it makes you feel any better, later in these shows, those kids get dragged off to boot camp by drill sergeants."

"Really?" Anthony asked with a newfound enthusiasm.

"Yes, sir. That's really the best part of the show. It's why they save it for the last part. Gets the viewers more amped up for when it happens."

"Well, we gotta keep watching now!"

And keep watching the two did. The host continued to interview the unruly teen for a few minutes. Then, she addressed the audience and the home viewers. "We've had the opportunity to talk to these out-of-control teenagers, and it seems that they're stuck in their ways and unwilling to change. But after the break we'll see if our special guests can break their destructive habits." The studio audience cheered loudly as the host pointed over to a curtain. The curtain showed silhouettes of three intimidating figures.

Anthony recognized the shape of the drill sergeant hats being worn by the three figures in the silhouettes. "OOOH, it's on now, boy!" Now he was more invested in the show than any other member of the family had ever been. He sprung up from his recliner as excited as a child attempting to jump from their swing in midair. "Imma go use the bathroom while the commercials are on. I don't wanna miss this!" He walked through the kitchen to the bathroom next to the laundry room. While doing so, he started to recite part of a military cadence he remembered:

"Now their backbones are hard as rock,

They can pump projos around the clock.

Load that projo and that powder,

Make that blast sound a little louder.

In the battle all will see,

The king of battle is Field Artillery."

Meanwhile, Will remained on the couch and watched the commercials on TV.

"FRIDAY FREAKFEST '99! The biggest party of the year is poppin' off in three weeks live from the Palisades Center in Fremont! With live performances from Ludacris, DMX, Jay-Z, Eminem, Busta Rhymes, and, fresh off of house arrest, local legend, Don Smurf!"

"Hey, it's your boy, Don Smurf, and Imma be at Friday Freakfest '99! Ladies, I just settled out of court with my baby mama, so I'm looking to see all y'all out there. So much so that I told them to let y'all in for ten dollars off if you buy your tickets now!"

"FRIDAY FREAKFEST '99! Tickets still on sale at all participating Shopmore locations or online at fridayfreakfest. com. Be there!"

The next commercial was far more conservative in theme. Stock business casual music played in the background while scenes of hectic downtown and office activity were being shown.

"For over fifty years, The Taylor Corporation has been at the forefront of innovation. We are the minds behind many of the advances in technology that are commonplace in the homes and lives of billions of people all over the world. And the Taylor Corporation will spearhead our world into the twenty-first century, working around the clock to further advance our innovations and creating new ones."

"Hello, I'm Donovan Taylor, president and CEO of TaylorCorp. As it was when my dear ol' daddy was in charge, and when grandpappy was before him, we work around the clock and around the world to bring you the latest and greatest in technology, from personal computers and the hardware and software that power them to everyday household items. And it is my solemn vow to you that we will continue to do so in the twenty-first century and even the twenty-second and twenty-third!"

"The Taylor Corporation, Innovating your tomorrow today! Find out more at taylorcorp.com."

That man on the television, Donovan Taylor, looked strangely familiar to Will. He wasn't absolutely sure, but Will thought that he was the same man who was speaking with Principal Caine in the office earlier. But before he could think too hard about it, the loud flush of the toilet his father was using derailed his train of thought.

Will's father returned to the living room still wiping his hands with a paper towel. He sat back down in his recliner and said to Will, "Woo, maybe your mama was right. Too much roast beef isn't good for ya. I wouldn't go in there for at least an hour. Did I miss it?"

"No, sir. It's about to come back on."

Will was right. The commercial break ended and the talk show resumed. "Now it's time to introduce these out-of-control teens to our special guests! Please welcome Staff Sergeant Lockett, Staff Sergeant Mugnaini and Sergeant First Class Rosa from the Hawks Ranch Juvenile Boot Camp!" The curtain was raised revealing two men and a woman dressed in full military uniform. They were far larger in stature and far more intimidating now that they were no longer hidden. The three drill instructors walked towards the stage and the teens as military themed music played in the background and the audience cheered uncontrollably.

Will's dad was leaning forward in his recliner. He was as excited as the show's studio audience, and he cheered on as if he were there among them. "See the one in the middle?" He asked Will. "I bet he was an airborne ranger." Anthony failed to guess the position of the female drill sergeant, but he was still impressed with how she was able to look and act as intimidating as her male counterparts. The three drill sergeants each singled out one of the guests and started barking orders at them.

"You like to fight?! Well, come on then! Hit me!" one of them screamed, egging his target on to strike him.

"For the next few days, I'm gonna be your mama and your daddy! Let me see you try to talk back to me!" another drill sergeant said to his target.

"So you like to drink, huh?" the last drill sergeant asked. "That stuff's nothing but empty calories. But don't you worry. We're gonna burn those off ASAP!"

This went on for about seven or eight minutes and both the audience and Will's father ate up and enjoyed every moment of it.

"All of you, stand up!" the drill sergeants ordered the guests. The guests stood up from their chairs. The sergeants then faced the audience. The two on the left and right side stood at ease while the one in the middle addressed the audience and the host.

"Jenny, in the next two days, we will instill discipline into these teens. They will return to their parents as well-behaved, respectful, and productive members of their households and their society!" The military-themed music played once again. The men turned again to the guests and gave orders to the teens to march in a single-file line to the backstage area.

Fifteen minutes later, the show ended. It was followed by another talk show. "Dashaniqua suspects her boyfriend Javarius of cheating on her with her sister, Quntashia. Is he? Stay tuned because the lie detector has all the answers!" These kind of shows would proceed each other long into the afternoon.

It was 4:30 in the afternoon before Will or Anthony knew it. Since Anthony's bathroom break, neither had left their seats, nor had they changed the channel. The quick beeps of the security alarm filled the house as the front door opened and Liz entered the house. Anthony looked to Will and sternly said, "Remember our deal, boy." Then he sprung from his recliner and met his wife halfway from the dining room to the living room with a romantic embrace.

A few seconds later, Liz made her way to the living room, where noticed Will sitting on the couch. "No booster club, today?" she asked him.

Will explained, "No, ma'am. We accomplished what we needed to do this week earlier than expected. So I was able to come home early. But I…uh…" He paused to look at Anthony who gestured at him to finish his confession. "I accidentally taped over your show."

With her arms crossed and a judgmental look on her face, Liz asked, "Which one?"

Will had to quickly think about which one of Liz's favorite shows came on at the time that he was in his room today. He knew it wasn't Oprah, which comes on last in the midday talk show rotation. Nor was it Jerry, which was on right now. Anthony and he spent the afternoon watching Jenny, Sally, and Ricki, so by process of elimination, Will answered, "Queen Latifah."

"Oh, that's okay, baby. Her show's gonna be nothing but reruns until next year," Liz responded.

While Will breathed a sigh of relief, Anthony's jaw dropped as he realized he had received the raw end of their deal. "I'm going upstairs to change, then I'll be down to get dinner started."

She began her ascent upstairs when Anthony asked her, "What are you cooking?" On the third step of the staircase, Liz looked over the banister and answered, "Food, honey. I'm cooking food."

The doorbell rang. Although he was closer to it than Will, Anthony was still sour and didn't feel like moving until he could get over the deal.

"Go see who's at the door," Anthony commanded.

Will got up from the couch and walked towards the front door. There, he proceeded to unlock the three locks and deadbolts that secured the door. Then he removed the stick-like apparatus that was attached to the doorknob that prevented anyone from turning it from both the inside and out. After the long process, Will opened the front door and saw both Nathan and Ashley standing on his porch.

"What's up, dude?" Nathan greeted.

Will poked his head out of the door and returned the greeting, "Uh…hey guys. How'd you know this is where I live?"

Ashley answered, "I looked up your address in the student database."

"How did you get into… You know what? Never mind. What are y'all doing here?"

"We couldn't find you anywhere at school today," Nathan answered. "We thought you might've been sick or something. So we came to check up on ya, dude."

At that point, Will could've explained what happened. He could've followed his father's advice and told them everything. About the past, about the nightmares, and how they affected him to the point where he finally lashed out earlier today. But he wasn't absolutely certain that the two would understand quite yet. So instead, he said to them, "You were right, Nathan. Too much of that cafeteria food is bad for you. But I had to eat breakfast. Whatever that stuff they served messed up my stomach something fierce, and the school nurse had to call my parents to come and pick me up. But I'm fine now. Thanks for checking up on me."

"No problem, dude. We're heading to the park down the road. You wanna come?"

Will hesitated to answer.

However, a loud voice from inside the house made his decision for him. "Hey, boy! You gonna be inside or out?! Either way, close my door! You letting out all the air conditioning!"

"To the park, then," Will answered.

The three headed to the park in the middle of Presley Place. While Ashley and Will walked, Nathan casually rode on his skateboard beside them.

"I looked further into that 'F2' thing," Ashley said out of the blue. "Between yesterday and today, there have been a whole lot more text messages being sent about it on campus."

"Any idea what it is yet?" Will asked.

"None," Ashley answered in a tone of disappointment. "The only thing I can say is that whatever it is, it was confirmed last night as you said. I even spent the entire night running web searches for 'F2.' But it's far too broad of a term. It would've been impossible for me to comb through millions of results and narrow it down in such a short time."

Ashley then raised her clenched fists in the air and roared, "ARRGH! I hate not having vital information! This could be the biggest thing to hit Washington, and after all this time, I'm still in the dark about it!"

"Whoa, calm down there, dude," Nathan intervened. "See, this is why we had to get you away from those computers for a while."

A few minutes later, the trio arrived at the Presley Place Park. Looking at it for the very first time since he moved into the neighborhood, Will stood in amazement at how massive it was. The freshly cut, green grass filled nearly every inch of ground in the vicinity. It had everything a standard park consisted of, including several fully equipped playgrounds and a basketball court surrounded by a steel fence. But there was so much more. Placed in the middle of a park was a beautiful circular fountain with a statue made of stone at its center. The fountain was surrounded by shrubs. In the distance there was a small building. In the rear of the building was a swimming pool that was fenced off for the season. Connecting each of the amenities in the park was a long, sidewinding path made of cement that was being shared by people walking, jogging, skateboarding, and riding bicycles. The path was wide enough so that no two people on it would clash with each other. In several locations along the path, there were benches where the older patrons sat, surrounded by well-maintained trees. There was also a section of the park dedicated to small tables where several people sat down to play checkers or chess.

"Pretty kick ass, right, dude?" Nathan asked the awestruck Will.

"It is. I've never been here before. My mother took my little sister here a few times, but her description failed to do it any justice," Will answered.

"Hmmph, another amazing perk of upper-middle-class living as afforded to us by the Taylor Corporation," Ashley added sarcastically. Her statement was backed up by the plaque placed on the fencing near the park's entrance. It was in a golden tint, and underneath the park's name, the plaque read, "A donation of the Taylor Corporation."

After her statement, Ashley walked off in a huff, still upset about not being able to figure out what "F2" was. Something in Will wanted to inquire if Ashley was feeling okay. He believed there had to be more causing Ashley to be upset than just not being able to crack that code. However, he didn't ask aloud; by the time he could express his concern, Ashley was well on her way to one of the swing sets. Nathan quickly patted Will on his shoulder and said to him, "Roll with me, dude."

Riding his skateboard, Nathan made his way to the paved pathway with Will following behind him with his hands in his pockets. Side by side, the two took up half of the pathway, leaving only the left side open for on-comers. Will looked around but couldn't see Ashley anywhere in sight. Now he wanted to ask about her; before he could, however, Nathan explained a few things to him.

"Her parents called her this morning. Said they'd be in meetings and conferences in New York for at least two weeks."

"Oh?"

"Yeah, dude. But this isn't anything new. They call, tell her where they're heading off to, put some money in her account, and just leave. It's par for the course, been like that for years. But the older she gets, the more frequent it's been happening."

"Hmm…"

"Look, dude. I know it looks like she puts on a tough face all the time, but that girl, she's been through a lot in the last year or so. See, dude, a mutual friend of ours—well, a former mutual friend, anyway—did something really crappy to us last year. I won't go into all the gruesome details, but Ashley never really got over it. She thought that girl was a real friend, someone she could place her trust into, something she doesn't do often, if at all.

"But that wasn't the case. Anyway, long story short, her pride was damaged a little, but her heart was hurt beyond repair. To make things worse, she really didn't have anyone she could go to for consolation. She didn't have other friends 'cept me because everybody thought she was weird for being all into computers and junk. And her parents? Well, they were at another one of their meetings in Hong Kong at the time. They didn't come back for another month."

This was a lot for Will to take in. Until this point, Will had speculated that his peers in the suburbs lived happy lives, that their only concerns were school and relieving their boredom. He thought that, as kind of an outsider, he was the only one with any real issues. And Nathan was right; if he hadn't told Will what happened to Ashley, he probably would've gone his entire life assuming that she was just some eccentric genius who found it easier to replace the people in her life with computers, similar to how he would block out people with music. He would've never guessed that she had some unresolved issues herself.

"Why are you telling me this?" Will asked.

"Two reasons, dude," Nathan answered. "First, because we friends gotta know stuff about each other. Like for instance, I haven't clipped my toenails in months! Yeah, dude, I saw some article in *National Geographic* of some old dude with the record for the longest toenails, and I thought to myself 'Man, I bet that guy gets all kind of chicks with those nails!'

"And secondly," Nathan continued. "Ashley trusts you, which, I've mentioned before, is rare. Remember when you two first met on Tuesday? Didn't go so well right? But she was able to conclude that you've lived a troubling life and are in desperate need for a friend or two, whether you agreed or not. So in a way, she could relate to you, dude, and I guess she figured she could place her trust in you."

"I…see," Will said hesitantly.

"Can she, dude?" Nathan asked him a tone more serious than ever before. "Can she trust you? Can she call you a real friend?"

Will didn't answer right away. He took a few moments to think about it as the two continued their trek along the pathway. Before he knew it, the two were on the other side of the park. Right across from them was another playground. This one was entirely empty, save for Ashley who was sitting on a swing with her back facing the boys. However, she wasn't alone from Will's point of view. The swing next to Ashley's was being occupied by the girl in the white dress facing in the same direction she was. Finally, Will answered, "Yeah, man. She can."

Will walked towards the swings while Nathan continued skating on the paved pathway. When he got closer to the swings, the girl in white faded away. He sat on the swing that was previously occupied by her. When he did, Ashley looked up and was shocked to see him sitting there. Will didn't say anything at first. He noticed the sullen look on Ashley's face as she looked down to the ground. In time and without any provocation, he started to talk.

"When I lived in Salem, I only had one friend. For a long time, I thought she only wanted to be my friend because she felt sorry for me. Turns out, she wanted me to have someone to talk to. And that's what we did for years; we talked. We talked about everything. She was always so cheery, so optimistic, so full of hope. It was irritating at times. I never figured out how she could find light in a place as dark as Salem. But I knew she was a really good friend. Unfortunately, I didn't realize it until it was too late."

"What happened?" Ashley asked.

Will sighed heavily and answered, "She passed away a few months ago. We were in a car crash, and she didn't make it. For the longest time, I blamed myself for her death. I had fully convinced myself that if I had been somehow able to alienate myself from her like I did everyone else, she'd still be alive today. I was so wracked with guilt that I could hardly eat or sleep for weeks. I was prepared to live the rest of my life in depression over it. But then you told me something that helped me, gave me some closure on it all. You said that no matter what the situation, I could get by with help from my friends. But that piece of advice. It works both ways, doesn't it?"

"Nathan told you about what happened last year, didn't he?" Ashley asked.

"Kinda. He didn't go into full detail. He spoke more about your parents than anything else," Will replied. "Thought it would only be fair that I'd spill my guts in return. Nathan says friends gotta know stuff about each other. Stuff you can't generally find on the student database."

Ashley's sullen look changed with a smile. "Yeah, it works both ways," she said in response to Will's earlier question. "Hey, listen, tomorrow night I want to show you something cool."

"Show me…something?" Will asked reluctantly.

"Yeah, it's a place Nathan and I hang out at times. Not too many people know about it. I think you'll really like it, and tomorrow night will be perfect to show it to you."

"Okay," Will said, accepting the offer.

Chapter Fifteen

Time passed on. The afternoon shifted into the evening. Will and Ashley remained on their swings in the playground while Nathan bounced around from place to place on his skateboard. He spent his time approaching both girls in his age range and older women, with varied results. Will and Ashley, on the other hand, spent their entire time together talking only to each other.

"You've lived in this neighborhood all your life?" Will asked.

"Yup. Born and raised here," Ashley answered.

"And you and Nathan?"

"Friends since kindergarten. Been through everything, thick and thin ever since. When his parents went through that nasty divorce, I was there for him. Just like he was for me when I lost my 'supposed' best friend last year."

As the two continued talking, Will felt something inside of him he hadn't in a while. It was a feeling of comfort. While he continued to listen to Ashley's words, Will envisioned the very last time he had sat with April on the swings at the park in Salem. However, something was a bit off. While he could remember that moment fondly, as if he was were experiencing it for the first time, he couldn't hear the words that April was saying. Her mouth was moving, sure, but it was Ashley's words that were coming out of it, accompanied with Ashley's voice.

Will tried to process what was happening. He took his right hand out of the pockets of his hoodie and used it to rub his forehead as if he were soothing a headache.

"Are you okay?" Ashley asked, stopping her previous conversation.

"I…uh…yeah, I'm fine," Will answered.

Just then, the two were joined by Nathan, who had completed his rounds around the park. "Dude, Miss Parker has still got it going on! You would never guess that she's going on forty-five! Can you believe that?! I bet they still card her for R-rated movies! I should go over to her house one day and ask her if she needs some yard work done or something."

Ashley jumped from off of her swing. She dusted herself off attempting to remove the dirt from the swing that had transferred to her clothing. "It's getting a bit late," she said. "Imma head home."

Nathan added, "I guess I should be going too. Miss Parker's done with her jog, so there's really no reason for me to be still be here."

Nathan and Ashley walked together towards the nearest exit. Will, on the other hand, remained, still sitting on his swing. He looked over to the now vacant swing with an inquisitive look on his face. "Where'd you go?" he asked seemingly to himself. He continued to look at the empty swing for a few moments, but he didn't receive an answer to his question. "Hmmm," he said with a scowl. He then leapt from his swing and proceeded to head home himself.

With his hands back in his pockets, Will walked back to his house. He fumbled his hands around a bit in his pockets. For some reason, he had forgotten that he didn't bring his CD player with him to the park, and he desperately looked for it as he walked. A few seconds later, he gave up in this endeavor.

Without music to drown them out, Will was exposed to the noises of the neighborhood; however, they weren't as bad to him as he had expected them to be. The sounds of the birds flying through the air as the slight wind wafted through; the cheers of small children as they played in both their yards and on the empty roads; the words exchanged by neighbors as they attempted to one-up each other with the boasts of new possessions and accomplishments—none of these were as bothersome as Will once perceived them to be. It was as if Will was finally starting to come to terms with the fact that this was his new home now, that was his new life.

Will made his way to Penley Avenue. He'd still have to cross the road of the cul-de-sac to get to his house. But as he started to, he was exposed to one more sound that he would have to become familiar with. Loud, rapid drumming noises came from the garage of the house that sat directly from his. The drumming was accompanied by even louder riffs from what sounded like an electric guitar. Will was by no means an expert in the art of rock music, but even he was able to deduce that the guitar playing was not in rhythm with the drumming.

Will started to cross the road. Halfway through, the drumming and guitar playing came to an abrupt end. It was replaced by the loud screams of a girl, "We're The Rock that Killed the Dinosaurs! Thank you and goodnight, Ingram Park!" Will didn't turn around to acknowledge the girl, he continued on to his house.

Inside the house, Will noticed his brother slumping on the floor of the living room with his hands behind him propping himself up and his eyes heavily glued to the television set. Will wanted to walk past him and head upstairs, but he was stopped midway. "Yooo! The Rock is gonna wrestle Triple H for the title tonight," DeMarcus said to Will.

"What are you talking about? Wrestling doesn't come on tonight," Will responded.

"You remember that SmackDown special from April? It came back on tonight. Big Bossman already beat Al Snow for the Hardcore belt, and Undertaker and Big Show defended their tag-team title in a triple threat," DeMarcus explained.

Obviously interested, Will postponed his plan to go upstairs to his room. Instead he sat on the couch, in the same place he had earlier, and joined his brother in watching the television. About fifteen minutes later, the main event that DeMarcus had alluded to started. The two watched with excitement. "C'mon, hit 'em with the rock bottom!" DeMarcus shouted.

"Oh no, he's gonna get hit with the pedigree!" Will added.

"Whew, thank God, he got out!" said DeMarcus.

The two boys took turns reacting to the action going on in the ring as if they were the commentators at ringside.

Midway through the match, the program cut to a commercial break. This gave the boys a chance to calm themselves from the excitement they had garnered from watching the match.

"Say, DeMarcus. What do you think about this place?" Will asked.

Without looking back at Will, DeMarcus answered, "What? Ingram? It's alright, I guess."

"You think it's better than Salem?"

"I mean… We could use some more bruthas and sistas up in here. But other than that, much better than Salem. You know, we been here for months already, and I ain't had to serve nobody with these fists yet. Feels good to just be able to chill and focus all my energy on what's really important, the females. And lemme tell ya, since most of them ain't seen a black dude outside of TV, they love me!"

"But you had a lot of friends back in Salem. You don't miss them?"

"Hell, no! Only reason why I was friends with most of them is 'cuz I thought, that way, they'd step off from messin' with you all the time. Them clowns weren't 'bout nothin'. I mean, they was cool in the beginning. But when we got older, they only thing they wanted to talk about and do was the same dumbass stuff their brothers and cousins and uncles got sent up north for. On top of that, I got tired of gettin' whoopin's from hangin' out with them and gettin' in trouble all the time while their parents let them run around and do whatever. So screw them! Only thing that matters is that we're here now!"

"Uh…right. That's uh…all that matters," Will replied reluctantly. He got up from the couch and started to head upstairs after all.

"You ain't gonna watch the end of the match?" DeMarcus asked, finally turning back to look at Will. Will didn't answer his question.

Inside his bedroom, Will turned on the light and went for his backpack sitting in the corner. He opened it and fished for the old notebook and flipped to the pages that held the photo of him and April from earlier in the year. He took out the photo, which was slightly covered in splotches of paint along its edges. With the photo in his hands, he sat on his bed and stared at the photo. "Where are you?" he asked. A few seconds passed. Still holding the photo, Will fell back onto his bed and closed his eyes.

***

The sun was brighter now than it had been all year. There were hardly any clouds in the sky to eclipse it. Summer had arrived, and it could be felt all around, from the brisk breeze to the ever-increasing heat. "It's ninety degrees out here. Aren't you hot in that thing?" April asked Will, referring to the hoodie he was wearing.

"Not really," he answered. "I actually like it when it's hot outside."

April could only laugh as her body movement swung the swing she was sitting on back and forth a bit. "I don't know if your parents are going to let you wear that on your birthday. It's coming up soon, right?"

"Two days," he answered.

"How's it feel to be turning fourteen?"

"Don't know. I'll say one thing, though. It's gonna be weird still sitting on these swings. We have to be getting too old to be playing on these by now."

"But this is where we always talk."

"Yeah, I know."

April reached down into her backpack that sat on the left of her. She opened it and pulled out a medium-sized object covered in a decorative gift wrap. "Here," she said presenting the object to Will. "I know it's early, but I wanted you to have this."

Will took the object and thanked April for it. He carefully unwrapped the gift, revealing a thick, hardcover book. Will's eyes lit up when he discovered what the book was. "*Watership Down?!*" he asked with excitement.

"I remember you saying it was one of your favorite books of all time and that your baby sister accidentally ruined your softcover copy when she was teething," April said.

"I've been looking for another copy for years! Thank you!"

"You're welcome," April responded with a warm smile.

Some time passed, and the two were still sitting on the swings together. "I overheard my parents talking the other day. They were talking about your dad and the job he may get with

TaylorCorp. If he gets it, you guys are going to have to move away."

"I…uh…" These were the only words Will could say in response.

"It's okay. I knew this would happen eventually."

"What?"

"You leaving Salem. I knew it would happen someday. You kept telling me how hard your dad had been working for that job. How he'd take classes for his certification during the day and work at night. I knew you weren't meant for this place. I always said you were going to do great things. And you definitely aren't going to do them here."

"But what about you?! It's not fair that I gotta leave you. I don't want to!"

"Oh, Will. I'll always be there with you, no matter what."

Will had a sat at his swing with a confused look. He hadn't the foggiest idea as to what April meant about always being there. How could she be, if the two were going to be cities, even states apart from one another?

"I want you to make me a promise. I want you to promise that no matter what happens, no matter where you go, or how far apart we may be, I want you to promise me that you'll live."

Once again, Will wasn't sure what April's words meant. "But I am living, April," he rebutted.

"That's not what I mean," she said. "Yes, you are alive, but I want you to actually live your life. Don't be afraid to do things, and don't just automatically shut people out and assume the worst of them. Live! Do you promise to do that?"

"Sure," Will answered softly, but not sincerely.

April removed her right hand from the chain binding the swing and reached out to Will, extending only her pinky finger. "Do you pinky swear?" Will looked up and saw the broad smile on April's face as she waited for him to commit to the pinky swear. He extended his left hand out to interlock his pinky finger with hers.

"Yeah, I pinky swear."

As their pinkies interlocked, the bright blue skies turned into a grim shade of grey and became filled with thunder and lightning. The light breeze became a steady rush of violent winds. Will and April looked up and saw the heavy rain coming down from the skies. They each jumped from their swings and backed away from the swing set in a frightened state. The winds picked up; they became strong enough to unearth the swing set and whisk the entire thing far into the unseen distance.

"Are you okay?" Will asked April.

"Yeah," she responded. "But we gotta get outta here!"

The thunder roared and lightning struck in rapid succession. Will could see the fear in April's eyes as she gasped. He couldn't recall the last time he'd seen that side of her, or even if he had at all. She got behind Will and clutched onto his arm while the two made their way through the storm. The rain obstructed his view quite a bit, but Will could see a shadowy figure approaching April and him. The figure came closer and closer to the two. It was another younger version of Will. He was dressed in a pitch black hoodie and looked to be eleven years old.

His had his hood up, covering most of his face in the process, and had his hands in his pockets.

"YOU! What are you doing here?!" Will screamed at his younger self loud enough to break through the sound of the heavy rain.

"I am reminding you of who you really are, since you're so adamant in denying it."

"What are you talking about?!"

"You? Me? We are burdens. We bring suffering and misery to everyone foolish enough to want to be around us. Because misery is the only emotion we have ever experienced."

The ground beneath Will and April began to shake violently. Then, it started to crack and crumble. Afterward, pieces of the ground broke off from one another, falling into what appeared to be a pitch dark void beneath the two. Will and April attempted to escape the quake, but the ground right underneath April fell into the abyss below.

"APRIL!" Will shouted. She was able to grab onto the next ledge of ground. Will ran back to her and grabbed one of her arms in an attempt to help her back to her feet. Will desperately struggled to lift April, but it was to no avail. His hands had become slippery due to the constant downpour. On top of that, April was much heavier than she appeared to be for some reason. No matter how much strength he could muster into both of his arms, she wouldn't budge.

"C'mon, April! Get up!" Will continued in his vain attempt to help April. "Please! Please get up!" Will pleaded with a mixture of sweat and tears running down his face. But April would still not budge. Will looked down and could not possibly be prepared for what he would see.

April was looking down at the void with an expression of lifelessness that Will would have never thought he'd see on her. April then looked back up at Will with the same lifeless look. She intentionally freed herself from Will's grip with ease, forcing him to fall on the fragile ground. Her limp body fell into the darkness. Her eyes never strayed away from Will. She uttered only one word as she fell: "Live."

April completely faded into the darkness. The sounds of thunder and rain were replaced with the sound of loud honking followed by the violent sounds of a car crashing.

Still on the broken ground, Will continued to look down in dismay. His arms and palms remained wide open; he couldn't believe that April would just let go like that. The younger Will stood over his counterpart on the still stable ground. "You tell yourself sweet little lies to get through each day. But every time you close your eyes, the truth will always be here to remind you. Remind you that you will only bring misery to those foolish enough to care about you. That is all we are. That is the truth. Now accept it!" the younger Will screamed as the thunder roared nearby.

Still looking down into the void that swallowed April, Will did the unexpected. He began to laugh. Quietly at first, but, in an instant, his laughter became more profuse.

"W-what are you laughing at? What's so funny?" the younger Will asked.

Will stood up on the broken platform, then turned around and climbed up to the stable ground. As he did this, the younger Will took a few steps back to distance himself from his older self. Will answered, "The fact that you thought I'd fall for that. That's what's so funny."

"Heh…It's just like I said. You're so miserable that you don't even show an ounce of concern or sadness when someone you claim you care about falls to her death."

"Do you think I'm stupid?" Will rebutted. "I know that wasn't the real April. For all her nagging about how great I was going to be and how I shouldn't give up, I know for a fact that she wouldn't just succumb like that. That she wouldn't just deliberately fall like that. Besides, do you really think she's gone for good?"

The younger Will grew angrier and angrier over Will's revelation over time. He furiously flung back the hood from over his head, revealing his eyes, bloodshot with rage. "Of course, she's gone! We watched her die! We were the cause, remember?!"

"That's what you've been wanting me to think all this time. And for a while, I did. But she isn't gone. She speaks to me, but not from my mind like where we stand now." Will put his hand on the left side of his chest, exactly over his heart, and continued, "She speaks to me from here."

The younger Will had reached his breaking point. With his fists clenched, he ran back towards Will screaming, "SHUT UP! SHUT UP! SHUT UP! SHE'S GONE! WE KILLED HER! AND WE'LL HURT EVERYONE THAT COMES NEAR US UNTIL WE ARE FINALLY ALL ALONE!" When he was within close range of Will, he lunged forward, attempting to land a fierce punch onto Will's face. But the attempt was met with failure. The younger Will's entire arm seemed to have just passed right through Will, as if he lacked a physical form. The rest of his body followed his arm as he rolled onto the ground behind Will.

"How?!" The younger Will asked. "How is this possible?!"

Without turning around to face his junior, Will explained. "Thanks to her, I figured it out. You are a part of me, there's no denying that. But all you are is the culmination of all the negative thoughts and feelings built over time from years of bullying and harassment from those who hated me."

"I am the truth! I am the feelings you have about the world and everyone in it!" the younger Will fired back.

"You were, once upon a time. But now, you're nothing more than a bully, seeking to make my life miserable because you can't find your own happiness. Seeking to drag me down just like they did because deep down, I knew wanted to do more, to be more, and they wouldn't accept that. And so, I'm doing what everyone who has ever cared about or loved me has told me to do when it comes to a bully, I'm ignoring you. And eventually, you will go away."

Will finally turned around to witness his negative self gasp in unmitigated terror as his body started to fade into the winds, from the bottom up. Eventually, his entire being was swept away in the now calming winds. The last drops of rain fell from the sky, and the sun broke through the dark clouds, exposing Will to the light once again.

Will placed his hand over his heart again and said, "I knew you weren't gone. It's like you said, you'll always be here with me." Just then, a voice that seemed to have come for the heavens called out to him. It was faint at first, but the voice became clearer as it called his name time and time again.

Chapter Sixteen

"Will!"

Will nearly sprung from his seat as his eyes opened in shock. He looked over to his immediate left to see Nathan waving his hands in an attempt to get his attention. "H-huh?" Will answered Nathan.

"Which one, dude?"

"W-wh-what are we talking about?"

Friday, August 27, 1999

Will and Nathan were sitting near the end of the fifth row of a set of bleachers in the newly added second gymnasium at Washington High. They were sharing these bleachers with almost the entire student body, most of whom were decked in green and gold apparel and accessories. There wasn't a single empty seat whatsoever. Every student in the stands looked towards the middle of the gym with anticipation.

They applauded and cheered along as the Washington High varsity cheer squad performed their signature routine on a large green platform that was slightly elevated from the floor. This platform was being occupied by Vice-Principal Terrell, Principal Caine, the coach of the football team, and several members of the booster club including Drew. Last and certainly not least, among these individuals was somebody donning the costume of a cartoonish-looking, green and white eagle wearing a green jersey with the letters "WHS" on the front.

The cheerleaders were those to whom Nathan was referring when he snapped Will back to reality in order to make a choice. "I'm digging the brunette at the left end. Woo, look at them thighs," he said with a brazen grin as he pointed toward her. "Now, which one do you like, dude? Which one's the hottest?" he asked.

Will was still opening his eyes, but even still, he could barely distinguish one cheerleader from the rest of her squad. Of course, they were all wearing the same uniform. It consisted of a V-neck, long-sleeved top with a design of green and gold coloring and the word "Eagles" written across their chests in a decorative golden cursive lettering surrounded in white. The A-line skirt, which almost touched their knees, was almost entirely green; two golden lines ran horizontally across the skirt's bottom. Their outfits were completed with all-white tennis shoes; if they were even wearing socks underneath, no one could see them. They all performed their routine with green and golden pom-poms in both of their hands. In fact, the only distinguishing factor between the girls was the color of their hair. Save for one redhead positioned in the rear of their formation, they were all either blondes or brunettes. Those with longer hair had it wrapped in a ponytail, adorned in a decorative bow with gold coloring.

To answer Nathan's question, Will pointed to one of the cheerleaders, almost entirely at random, and answered, "Uh… that one," with uncertainty.

"Whoa, dude! I mean, I don't judge. If that's what you're into, then more power to you."

Will had absolutely no idea what Nathan was talking about.

To finish their routine, the cheerleader in the middle of the formation, presumed to be their leader, bent one knee while still standing, stretched out her arms to her sides and proclaimed, "Go Eagles Go!" as loud as she could. This was met with thunderous applause from the students in the bleachers all across the gym. Afterward, the squad moved towards the back end of the platform. Taking their place with a microphone in his hand, Drew from the booster club addressed the crowd.

"Let's hear it one more time for our Washington High varsity cheer squad!"

The crowd resumed their applause, now louder than before. This went on for about another minute.

Drew continued, "Now, the moment you've all been waiting for. Let's give it up for…"

Drew was interrupted by Claudia, the secretary, who ran from one of the gym's entrances to hand him a small piece of paper. Drew began to read from the paper with less enthusiasm than previously, "The owner of a white Toyota Tercel in the senior parking lot whose lights are on."

"Ah, dammit!" said a voice from the stands that could be heard by everyone due to the crowd now being silent. A boy struggled to work his way to the end of the row of bleachers and then run down the stairs and out of the gym.

"Okay then," Drew said. He crumbled up the slip of paper and placed it into Claudia's hand. Then he dismissed her from the stage with a wave of his free hand. Back at his previous pitch and tone, he continued, "Let's give it up for your Washington High Eagles!"

Electronic music played from the huge speakers positioned at both corners of the further end of the platform. It was loud, but nowhere nearly as loud when compared to the roar of the crowd as members of the varsity squad came to the stage one-by-one from the boys' locker room. The team members were wearing the top portion of their uniform, green jerseys with bright gold lines going across both the V-neck and the bottom of the sleeves. The front of the jerseys read, "Washington," in standard gold athletic type; below the school's name sat the player's number in gold with a white trim around it. On the upper back of the jerseys, there was each player's last name in gold with his number once again underneath. Along with the uniform, their lower body apparel varied from shorts and sweatpants to jeans.

One of the players making his way to the platform was Eddie, Krystal's boyfriend, who had given Will a ride home a few days prior. His appearance was met with loud cheers from Krystal which could be heard from halfway across the gym.

After each member of the team took his place on the platform and the applause died down, Drew handed one of the players, likely the captain of the team, the microphone. "Washington High! This is our year! This is the year we take it all the way to state, all the way to the championship! This is the year we crush any and every team that we face!"

The crowd applauded yet again. The captain resumed his passionate speech with, "But you don't need to take my word for it! That's right, Washington! You've been waiting for this moment for long enough! Fresh off of last year's academic probation, I give you The Tank!"

Another player joined the team. He was so tall that his head nearly touched the top of the double doors leading to the locker room. He was so muscular that his body mass nearly covered the entire doorway. As he slowly made his way to the platform to join his teammates, music similar to that found in movie scenes where barbarians and other warriors clashed in battle played from the speakers. To Will it sounded similar to the music that played when the pro wrestler Bill Goldberg made his way to the ring. The crowd pounded their fists in the air and chanted his moniker, "Tank! Tank! Tank!" with enough energy amongst them to power a small city.

Tank snatched the microphone from the captain's hand and began his speech to the overhyped crowed. As if he were standing in the middle of a wrestling ring cutting a passionate promo, he made a proclamation: "Tonight is only the beginning! Week after week after week, we will march onto the field of battle and clash with the lowly mortals you refer to as our rivals! And, like the mighty eagle of our namesake, we will prey upon them like the helpless fish they are!" The crowd started a different chant of "Eagles! Eagles! Eagles!"

Tank finished his speech with, "Yes! I learned what they eat in biology class!"

Will rose from his seat in the bleachers as the crowd continued to chant and cheer.

"Where are you going, dude?" Nathan asked still seated.

"I've had more than my fill of school spirit for one day. I'm going to the library to see what Ashley's up to," Will answered.

Like the boy from earlier, Will squeezed through the students in the bleachers to make his way to the nearest exit. When he finally got to the stairway leading to the floor, Will placed his hands into his hoodie pockets and continued to exit the gym. While he was doing so, one of the cheerleaders took possession of the microphone.

"Okay! Let's see who can cheer on our boys the loudest! Freshmen, make some noise!" All of the freshmen scattered throughout the crowd cheered as loud as they could. Still walking to the exit, Will took brief notice that several of the students who weren't cheering were looking around and tapping away at their mobile phones. After the cheers of the freshmen died down, the cheerleader told the sophomores in the crowd to cheer. This was followed by the juniors and then, finally, the seniors.

Will walked across the campus towards the B building and the library. There were a few students hanging outside of the cafeteria area, taking advantage of homeroom classes being cancelled for the pep rally. None of them seemed to be the types that had any school spirit in them. During his trek, Will also took notice of the lack of security guards on campus as a whole. There were only one or two in the gym, and Will only saw one more patrolling the campus during his walk.

The library was even emptier than the rest of the campus. The librarian's desk was vacant, and there was nobody within the bookshelves. The lights on the second floor weren't even on. It seemed that Ashley was completely by herself, save for Will, who approached her at the desk she normally occupied. Rather than tap on her shoulder, he walked up to the computer next to her.

"Hey," Will greeted.

"Hey, yourself," Ashley returned. "Thought you were at the pep rally with Nathan."

"Hmm. I'm as pepped as I'm gonna get for a game I'm probably not going to."

"It's probably for the best. Can't understand how the school can get excited for a team that hasn't won more than three games a season for the last five years."

"Really? But they've got that really big guy now, The Tank."

"So? They've got a good defensive line, but it doesn't mean jack if their offense is garbage that can't put any points on the board. All the opposing team has to do is get within field goal range and they can nickel and dime their way to victory."

Will looked at Ashley, as she continued staring at the monitor and typing away on the keyboard, with surprise and amazement that she knew what she did about football. Without looking back up at him, Ashley could sense the bewilderment Will harbored. "A few years ago, my parents dragged me to a Super Bowl party their colleague was hosting. Someone explained the entire game to me and, as I like to do, I retained the knowledge to this day," she explained.

"Um…okay. Are you still running that text message program?"

"Yeah. I thought I'd run one more search on 'F2.' The texts seem to have died down today. Some of them popped up a few minutes ago saying things along the lines of 'They just marked themselves' and 'They made themselves known.'"

"What does that even mean?" Will asked.

"I have no idea!" Ashley responded throwing her arms up in the air in defeat. "Argh! If I could see the phone numbers or names of the people these texts are coming from!" Ashley started furiously clicking away on the mouse beside the keyboard and pounding keys on the keyboard.

"What are you doing now?" asked Will.

Ashley leaned a bit to the right and used her right arm to prop her head up. She answered, "I'm putting this program on the back burner for a while. I might just scrap it altogether. It's time I start writing a new one." A distinct growling noise came from Ashley's stomach. "But I ain't writing one line of code without any muffins! Damn it, Nathan! You just had to rush to school to get good seats; you just had to stare at those cheerleaders from the 'perfect view!'"

✳✳✳

The campus was filled with hectic activity throughout the day. Students moved around at a frenzied pace between class periods.

Not only were most of the students excited for tonight's football game, but they were also linking up with their various social circles, making and confirming plans for the weekend. Despite the chaos that filled the halls and corridors during these times, Will still noticed a severe lack of security officers and disciplining administrators.

For the most part, the classes themselves were a serene endeavor. Will was able to make amends with his biology teacher for yesterday's altercation during first period. While he didn't take the time to explain the cause of his tardiness and negative attitude to her, he assured her that it probably wouldn't happen again, which seemed to satisfy her. During second period, Will tried to pay attention to his algebra teacher's lecture while ignoring Nathan's constant insistences that he check out the girl who sat in front of him.

Rather than meeting up in the library as usual, Will, Ashley, and Nathan shared lunch with each other at one of the small tables outside of the cafeteria. There was no way they were going inside the cafeteria proper. It was filled with applause for the football players who occupied their normal table. Everything the athletes did, from flexing their muscles, to crushing milk cartons over their heads, to harassing the more meek passers-by, was met with thunderous applause from the students in the cafeteria.

Later in the day, Will continued his painting of the girl in the dress who followed him on and off again throughout the week. Ms. Johansen navigated around the circle made of her students and their canvases and made more observations of their work.

"Ah, William. I see that is coming along quite nicely," Ms. Johansen complimented. There was paint on the canvas, true, but Will was by no means a skilled painter. The average eye would not have been able to interpret what he was trying to paint. Ms. Johansen, however, was able to make something out of the disarray that was Will's painting. "Is it safe to assume that you are able to put the pieces of that puzzle together after all?" she asked him.

He answered, "I was able to find some pieces underneath the sofa. It's not complete, but I'll put together the pieces I have now."

Only one more period separated Will from the freedom of the weekend: history class. With a copy of the assigned textbook his hand, Mr. Carlisle casually leaned across the front of his desk as he had on the first day of school and spoke to the class.

"Now, we know there were a lot of famous historical figures present at the signing of the Declaration of Independence, but not all of them put their name on the document. One of these men was one of the Seven Founders of Ingram. For five bonus points on your first exam, who can tell me which one it was?"

None of the students raised their hand to answer Carlisle's question; either they didn't know the answer, or they didn't want to answer it. So the teacher picked on one of the students to answer instead.

"How about you, Mr. Moon?" he beckoned. Without hesitation or second-guessing himself, Will answered, "Addison Taylor."

"Correct," Carlisle said with a surprised tone. "The forefather of the CEO of TaylorCorp, to whom many of your lifestyles are owed, was present at the signing. But he didn't sign. Why is that? Even to this day, the answer to that question is a mystery wrapped in controversy. And you will all be learning that controversy and the Taylor legacy have gone hand-in-hand as we begin our unit on westward expansion."

The bell rang, and Mr. Carlisle dismissed the class for the day. "Okay, you kids. Go do weekend stuff. But remember, your first quiz is on Tuesday, so think about how you spend your time." For the most part, the students ignored his words. "We only go around once! Don't waste single minute on regret!" he shouted with excitement as the class had already exited the room.

Will exited the classroom last and found himself in a remotely empty hallway. He figured his peers were so excited for the weekend that they must've run to the exits of the campus. He started to put in one of his earbuds. But before it even touched his ear, he paused as he heard a loud slamming noise in the distance. He froze in his tracks as the noise grew louder and drew nearer. He turned his head in the direction the noise was coming from to see two older boys, one tall and one portly, walking toward him holding metal trash cans. In repetition, they slammed the lids against the cans. Finally, one of them yelled at the top of his lungs, "Freshmen! Come out and plaaaaaay!"

Chapter Seventeen

One of the two boys heading towards Will with trash cans in hand pointed at him and said to the other, "There's one! Get him!" They started to run towards Will, still slamming the lids against the cans.

With no one else in the hallway as far as he could tell, Will concluded that the two boys were referring to him and began to flee from his pursuers. He didn't even put his earbud back into his hoodie pocket, so it dangled back and forth against his leg as he ran.

There was a bit of distance between Will and the boys, but that gap became smaller and smaller with time. Fortunately, before the two could catch up to Will, the bigger of the two had to stop to catch his breath, allowing Will to successfully flee. Will slammed through the double doors leading to the outside walkway. In front of him stood another older student cornering a freshman on one end and two more trapping him from the other end next to a green plastic garbage container far larger than the one held by the boys from before. It was filled to its brim with trash.

With no other choice, Will crept up closer on the students who were completely occupied with closing in on the freshman. Upon closer view, Will saw that the target in question was none other Rob. His hunters were the three boys that had harassed him twice before in the week.

"We told you, you were going to get what's coming to you!" one of the boys said as the trio closed in on Rob even more. Will ran in to ambush the one standing on his end. Will ran past the boy to Rob, bumping into him with his shoulder with enough force to make the boy fall onto the ground. "Hey look, it's his 'homeboy'! Let's get him, too!" said one of the still standing boys on the opposite end.

Before the two could grab Will or Rob, Will took Rob by the wrist and doubled back towards the building he had just left. However, they did not re-enter the building. Instead they circled around the outside wall of the building. During their escape, both Rob and Will took note of the chaos taking place throughout the campus exterior. All throughout on both stories of the campus, freshmen were being chased by the older kids. When caught, they were subjected to all methods of hazing including being dunked into trash cans, pantsed, and given painful wedgies. Some students were being led, carried even, into the nearest building. For what reason, Will didn't want to know.

"Will, what's goin' on, fool?!" Rob asked while the two continued to run and avoid older kids.

"I don't know," Will answered, "You okay, though? Those clowns didn't do anything to you, did they?"

"Naw, but they was real close, though! If you ain't show up to…Wait! I thought we wasn't homies no more! Then you run up and save me? You tryin' to say I'm some mark ass busta that can't look out for himself?!"

"What? No! Look. I was having a bad day yesterday, and I took it out on you for no reason. I'm sorry for that. We're still homies, Rob."

"Whew, 'cuz, man, I was about to say. I ain't wanna have to start no beef with you on campus. A turf war ain't good for either one of us, know what I'm sayin'?"

"I never do! But let's worry about getting out of here for now!"

"Fo' sho', homie!"

The two made it to another walkway that connected the building. They took advantage of it being empty at the time and ran across, entering the building of the library. The building was far too quiet for Will's liking. He signaled to Rob to follow his lead and tread lightly through the hall. Up ahead, Will could see the motions of shadows of other students. The hunt had made its way into the library building.

At that moment, Will and Rob felt hands placed on one of their shoulders. The two looked at each other in absolute fear as they both thought they were finally caught by the older kids. "Oh, God, please don't let these fools kill us!" Rob pleaded in fear, still not sure who was behind Will and him.

"Get in here, dudes," a voice quietly said to them. It was that of Nathan, who lead them inside the nearby janitor's closet.

Will and Rob joined Nathan inside the janitor's closet. With all of the cleaning supplies on the shelves and the floor, it looked like it was barely suitable for one person for a long period of time, let alone the four that would occupy it for the next few minutes. Already inside was Ashley, squatting in the corner and rubbing her forehead with both hands in both fear and disappointment.

"What's going on, Nathan?" Will asked.

"Shh, dude," Nathan said quietly as he reached over to cover Will's mouth. With his free hand, he pointed at the vents on the bottom of the door, through which Will could see several pairs of legs walking by. After the people outside had walked by, Nathan explained the situation.

"Dude, you remember that hazing thing my dad was talking about the other day? The one he said they banned a few years back?"

"Yeah, why?"

"This is it. All the juniors, seniors, and even a bunch of the sophomores banded together to bring it back! My dad was able to remember the name of it. He was talking in his sleep. It's called Freshman Friday."

"Freshman Friday. F-F. Or F2," Ashley added. "That's what they've been talking about in those text messages all week. That's why nobody said anything about it in person. Arrgh! How could I not figure that out?! How could I be so dumb?!"

"Chill, Ash!" Nathan said. "It's not your fault. You two were out there. How's it look?"

"Like a damn warzone, fool!" Rob responded. He was answered with hushes from the other three, reminding him to keep his voice down. More quietly, he continued, "They all over the place snatchin' people up."

"He's right," Will added. "They're running in both small- and large-scale groups, too. It's chaotic but organized at the same time."

Ashley stood up and said, "Of course, they've been planning this all week, picking their spots. The texts from this morning? They pretty much ID'd all the freshman at the pep rally. On top of that, they're taking full advantage of the security being more lax due to the whole drug search debacle. Whatever security and administrators are left on campus now can't possibly bust them all. I'm sure Caine will have some punishment lined up for them next week, but that's not going to help us now."

"She's right, dudes," Nathan said. "Right now, we gotta get off campus. Dad that's the only way you can escape Freshman Friday."

"But yo, how we supposed to do that, huh?" Rob asked. "They got this whole place on lock, and you know they got the front gate and the parking lots hemmed up tight."

Nathan answered, "Through the practice field. There's a fence that we can climb over that leads right through the neighborhood next to the school."

"But how are we going to get there?" Will asked.

The group pondered the answer to Will's question for a few seconds. Meanwhile, another series of legs could be seen running past the door's vent. "I've got it!" Ashley said. Then she started to explain, "We need to get to the cafeteria. Then we'll make our way through the kitchen and out the service exit. From there we can cross over to the old gym and its rear exit out to the track and onto the practice field."

"Okay then, that's what we're doing," Nathan said with approval. He shifted himself past Will and Rob and slowly cracked the door open. He didn't see anyone coming from either end of the building, so he motioned for the rest of the group to follow him.

With Nathan as their leader, the four made their way back out. They took extra precaution not to gain the attention of anyone, friend or foe, as they made their way to the cafeteria. Their escape, thus far, was successful. They managed to enter the cafeteria although it didn't provide any sanctuary from the hazing. Ahead of the group, more students were being dunked into large garbage bins inside. These were filled with discarded food and drink of all varieties. One of the students performing the hazing turned around, thinking he had heard the footsteps of someone trying to escape his wrath, but he saw nothing. Nathan and the rest were able to duck underneath the circular tables in the nick of time.

On each of Nathan's signals, the others followed him, crawling from table to table until they reached the table closest to the bussing station. Nathan pointed towards the door leading to the inside of the station and quietly said, "Okay, dudes, that's our way out."

"But that door's gotta be locked," Ashley objected.

"I know. So you three are gonna stay here until I give the signal."

"Nate…wait!" Ashley said, but not soon enough. Nathan crawled from under the table and walked to the bussing station. He climbed onto the immobile conveyor belt, where trays and dishes were normally placed, and shifted his body through the small but long window leading to the kitchen area. Meanwhile, Rob took this break from running to introduce himself to Ashley.

"What's up wit' you, ma? I'm Rob, by the way. My homies call me Big Rob Dawg, but you can call me your little white chocolate drop." Will rolled his eyes and shook his head.

Ashley responded with, "I know who you are, Robert. We had band class together in junior high, remember? You still play that clarinet?" Will covered his mouth to conceal the small snicker he made in response to this revelation.

"Man, shut up!" he told Will. "I sold that thing for all this fly gear I'm rockin'! I ain't no clarinet-playin' scrub!"

A few moments later, a door nearby opened and Nathan stood there signaling the other three to join him. One by one, they joined him in the kitchen. It was entirely empty. The staff had all gone home for the day. They all headed towards the service door as planned and back outside to the rear portion of the campus. With no one in sight, the group scurried across the paved pathway to the old gym.

Immediately to the right of the entrance of the gym was a set of double doors leading to the basketball court and the exit the group would need to get to. Before any of them opened the doors, Nathan stood on his tip toes to look through one of the small windows on the top of the doors. "Aw, crap, dudes!" he said.

"What?" asked Will.

Without immediately answering, Nathan took Ashley by the hand and led her down the small hallway to the locker room while Rob and Will followed suit. The group met on a bench between a set of lockers where Nathan told them what he witnessed.

"They've got a whole bunch of freshmen lined up against the wall and they're just pelting them with dodgeballs!"

A frenzied Rob said to the others, "Damn! Ain't no way we gonna get past them suckas now! That's it, man! Game over, man! Game over! I say we just go up in there and get our licks and be done with it! Y'all got me out here runnin' like the cops is coming for us and we all got warrants. Yo, real talk? These boots ain't made for runnin'!"

Ashley and Nathan tried to calm Rob down as to not gain an attention from anyone else who might have been in the locker room. Meanwhile, with his hands in his pockets, Will got up from his spot on the bench and sternly said to the others, "I'll lure them out."

"Huh?" Nathan asked.

"Look, you guys stick to the door of the locker room behind me. I'll head inside the basketball court and provoke them to chase me outside of the gym. When you see me do that, you guys head inside and continue your escape."

"But they'll catch you for sure. And God knows what they'll do to you when they do," Ashley rebutted.

"I know they will. But hopefully it'll take so long for them to do so, that it'll buy you guys the time you need to get off campus. Now follow me."

Now with Will at the lead, the group exited the locker room. As instructed, Nathan, Ashley, and Rob remained near the doorway and watched as Will put in his earbuds, turned on his CD player and made his way inside the basketball court. It was as Nathan described. Several freshmen were lined up against the nearby wall and were being assaulted with a flurry of dodgeballs by their seniors. When the volley was complete, the freshman against the wall were replaced with a new group, and the barrage began again.

"Hey, jackasses!" Will shouted loud enough that he could hear himself through the music, gaining the attention of everyone else on the court, most importantly the older kids. "Come get me!"

As he said they would, the older kids immediately dropped their dodgeballs onto the ground and gave him chase right outside, giving Nathan and the others the opportunity to escape.

With several of the other kids in hot pursuit, Will ran as fast as he could back towards the main campus. Those who began their chase of him from the basketball court were joined by even more students as he ran through the exterior pathways, gaining their attention as he did so. Will burst through the entrance doors of the closest classroom building. Ahead of him were some more students who were still hazing freshmen. He gained their attention as well. However, instead of turning around and running back the other way where he knew there would be a larger number of older kids awaiting him, he opted to run towards the three in front of him.

"How's this for living, huh? Is this what you meant by living? Am I alive yet? Well am I?!" It appeared that he was asking himself these questions as he ran; however, he was directing them at April in reference to the promise he had made to her.

Midway down the hall, Will took a detour up the stairwell leading up to the second floor. He thought this would give him more leeway and allow him to attempt to reunite with his friends. This action, however, instead led to his undoing. On both ends of the second floor, there were several older students, some of whom were pursuing him from the basketball court earlier. They had run around the building, re-entered it via another doorway, and taken another flight of stairs up hoping to cut him off. Will looked towards both ends and saw them both blocked off by students. He then looked back down the flight of stairs he had taken seconds ago to see a group of students blocking it off as well. With no other choice, he took out his earbuds, placed them back into his pockets and quietly raised both of his arms in surrender.

Three boys stepped out from the group standing in the north end of the hallway. It was the group that, at this point, Will was sure he and Rob had made mortal enemies of. The boy, who yesterday proclaimed that Will was going to "get what was coming to him," ordered, "Get him in there!" to the group on the opposite end. Several students from that group walked up to Will and one of them began to shove him forward. Will was then pushed into the bathroom with even more force than he had been by the security officer on Wednesday. Two larger students stood on each side of Will; each of them grabbed him by a forearm and led him into the middle toilet stall.

One of the students kicked open the door of the stall. Will was led into the stall and forced to his knees. Standing outside of the stall, the leader of the trio from before asked Will, "Got anything to say now, 'homie'?" Will didn't say anything in response. "Didn't think so. Dunk him," the boy commanded. The two on Will's sides did as ordered. One grabbed both of Will's arms to prevent any resistance. The other took Will by the back of his head and plunged it into the toilet water.

It had been years since Will had last swum in a pool. At this moment, he recalled when he was nine years old. His grandmother Josephine had hosted a family barbecue at her house. He didn't normally remember much of the event, but now he could remember one part of it vividly.

He remembered when he stood on the diving board of the backyard pool in fear. Not only was it his first time diving from it, but he had little to no experience in swimming in the pool's deep end. While his mother pleaded with him to get off of the board, the other attendees told him to hurry up and jump so that they could take their turns on the board. Finally, Will's dad joined him on the diving board, but he didn't escort him off of it. Instead, Anthony picked him up and threw him into the pool himself!

The force of the swimming pool's water as Will desperately tried to swim to the surface was as powerful as the jet stream of the flushed toilet water swirling around him now. This went on for a few seconds more as Will tried to breathe under the toilet water. Through the water, Will could hear the loud laughter of several of the students as they vacated the bathroom.

Now, with his hands free, Will propped himself out of the toilet bowl and headed to one of the sinks across the bathroom. He reached into the towel dispenser with his right arm to grab a few paper towels to wipe off his soaked head, but the dispenser was completely empty, and so was the one on his left.

Will looked down at his hoodie, which was also drenched with water from the neckline up. For a minute or two, he let a loud laugh, the first time he had genuinely laughed for so long. It didn't matter to him that he was just humiliated in front a considerable portion of the older members of the student body. Instead, he took satisfaction in the certainty that his sacrifice wasn't in vain, that the others had successfully fled the campus unscathed. Will took his CD player from the pockets of his hoodie and bent down to place it in his backpack. Then he took off the hoodie altogether, revealing the plain black T-shirt underneath, and used it to dry his head. He looked down at his hoodie one final time and said to himself, "What's past is past." He placed the hoodie into the large trash bin next to the sink and left the bathroom.

Chapter Eighteen

Walking back out to the hallway, and through the campus leading up to the front entrance, Will bore witness to the aftermath of Freshman Friday. Young students shifted their bodies in unusual ways in order to get out of the lockers they were stuffed into. Some attempted to rid their hair of the debris from the trash cans they were stuffed into, and others rearranged their underwear to its rightful position. A few more stood nearby to soothe the pain from the purple nurples and Indian rug burns they received. Will also saw a few older students being detained by the few administrators and security officers, but the number of those being detained paled in comparison to the number of students who took part in the hazing.

Will proceeded to walk home. On the main road, he moved his hands to his stomach region as if he was grabbing for the CD player he normally had stashed in his hoodie pockets. He paused on the sidewalk after realizing that he no longer had the hoodie and let out a short, quiet snicker. He pulled off his backpack, grabbed the CD player, and put in his earbuds. He turned on the CD player to the track entitled "Doomsday" by MF Doom. Though Will couldn't understand all of the lyrics, the instrumental of the track provided him with tranquility as he walked home.

Will arrived at the front gate of Presley Place. Without any trouble, he entered the correct code that opened the gate to the housing area. The welcoming sound that played from the keypad as the gate opened was the final confirmation that Will needed. This was his home now. This was his life now.

Will entered his house at around ten minutes till five. He walked into the living room to greet his mother, who was sitting on the couch reading a cooking magazine while the TV played in the background.

"What horrors are you subjecting us to tonight?" he asked sarcastically.

Liz answered, "Ha ha, very funny. You should write books with that sharp wit of yours. I was going to try this black bean soup, but wouldn't you know it? There's no cumin left on the spice rack. So how about pizza instead?"

Will suggested, "You should call Giuseppe's. They deliver quickly and they're really good. Some friends told me about the place."

"You…have friends?" Liz asked both skeptically and enthusiastically at the same time.

"Yes, ma'am. I'll introduce you to them one day, but for now I need to take a shower and change clothes. The…uh…football team thought it would be cool to dump a cooler of water on us Booster Club kids during the pep rally…some backwards tradition or something…"

"I was wondering what happened to that dingy hoodie you always wear."

Will responded to Liz's inquiry regarding his hoodie with more honesty than his previous statement. "Oh, I got rid of that thing. And I'm going upstairs to get the other hoodies out of my closet. You can either donate them to Goodwill, or I can trash them now." He made his way to the staircase and finished, "I'm done living in the past, Mom," as he headed upstairs. On the final stair, he shouted back down, "Seriously, though, call Giuseppe's!"

Later in the evening, Will came back downstairs at his mother's behest. As he said he would, he had showered and changed clothes. He was now wearing some of the clothes his mother had previously bought from Park Hills Mall including a V-neck, short-sleeved shirt with white, grey, and olive green stripes going down it and a crisp pair of midnight navy denim jeans. Will joined his family at the dinner table.

"Boy, this is some good pizza," Anthony complimented. "And they delivered it to the house, too? I'm telling y'all, this is the life!"

"Dang, Will. You actually look…halfway fly in them clothes. You lose a bet or something?" asked DeMarcus.

"No, just thought it was time for a change." Will answered plainly. Just as he was about to grab a slice of pizza from the large box in the middle of the table, the doorbell rang.

"Go get the door, boy," Anthony said to DeMarcus.

"Why I gotta get it? I'm eatin'. Make Will get it. He ain't even got a slice on his plate yet."

"Go get the door before I get the belt."

"Tch… Man, this some booty right here," DeMarcus said under his breath.

"What was that?" Anthony asked.

"Yes, sir," DeMarcus said with louder and with more clarity. He hopped up from his chair and made his way to the front door. Anthony shouted to him, "And if it's somebody selling something, you get the bat that's in the living room on 'em! I done told them kids we ain't buyin no magazine subscriptions. I don't care what space camp they tryin' to go to."

The beep of the security alarm filled the house, indicating that DeMarcus had opened the door. None of the other family members could hear what he was saying to whoever was at the door until he dramatically started yelling, "Oh, Lord, why?! Why they out here takin' all our sistas?! Why, Lord?! Why?!"

With the slice of pizza in his hand, a few seconds away from his mouth, Will sighed and said, "That's probably for me." He placed the slice back down on his plate and joined his brother at the front door.

"Get out of the way," Will demanded of DeMarcus. DeMarcus returned to the kitchen, freeing up the doorway and allowing Will to see that it was Ashley and Nathan who had rung the doorbell. Will joined the two outside, closing the door behind him. They were both standing beside mountain bikes.

"Dude, what happened?" Nathan asked.

"Exactly what I said would. But you should've been there. It took, like, thirty of them to corner me."

"Really?! That's badass, dude," Nathan responded with admiration.

"So, what did they do to you?" asked Ashley.

"The ol' swirly," Will answered. "Had to come home and take a shower. Was in there so long that my dad posted the recent water bill on the refrigerator and said I'd be paying it with the paycheck from my first job. But that's beside the point. Did you guys escape?"

"There wasn't anyone on the track or the field. We were able to get away scot-free, dude."

"Good, I'm glad. What's with the bikes?"

Ashley responded, "You remember that place I told you about yesterday? The one Nate and I hang out from time to time? We came over here to get you, to take you there."

"Gotta bike, dude?"

"Yeah, but I…uh…haven't ridden in a long time."

"You never forget, dude. Let's go now. We don't wanna miss it."

Will went back inside to inform his parents that he was going out with his friends for a while. A few minutes later, the electronic garage door opened, and Will walked back outside with a cherry red mountain bike. "Lead the way," he told the two.

Will followed Nathan and Ashley on their bikes to the entrance of Presley Place. When they were able to, they crossed over to Benbrook Street and then crossed right afterward. They rode on the sidewalk of York Road for about a mile until they reached a trail, built for walking and biking, on the right side.

The trio entered Westwood Trails and traversed the sidewinding gravel trail with relative ease, save for Will who spent a few moments getting reacquainted with the basics of riding a bicycle. Somewhere down the trail, the three crossed over a small, wooden bridge over the same brook that ran from Benbrook Street. A few minutes after crossing the bridge, Nathan and Ashley deviated from the gravel trail into the woodland area on its side. Will continued to follow, now a bit suspicious as to where this would lead.

The kids got off their bikes and leaned them against a nearby tree; the wheels became buried in the leaves that had been slowly falling from the trees in the past weeks.

"It's just up here, dude," Nathan said assuring Will that they wouldn't be going far from their bikes. There was a path leading to their final destination. It wasn't manmade in the same way as the gravel trail leading up to this point; it was a part of the ground that was made into a path from the many feet that had walked upon it over many years.

Will, Nathan, and Ashley exited the woodland area on the other side. They found themselves staring at a field of considerable size made of green grass that waved back and forth with the frail wind in the air. The sky had grown dark enough to bring out the stars that could not be seen while in the neighborhood. On the field stood a very tall oak tree on a highly elevated piece of land. The group traversed the field, climbing the hill to stand under the shade of the tree.

"What is this place?" Will asked with great interest.

Ashley explained, "It was on this very hill, that the Seven Founders of Ingram made the decision that this would be their new home. To commemorate this discovery, they planted this very oak tree, and named this spot Fate's Hill, because they thought their being here was a part of their destiny."

"Me and Ashley? We always come out here, dude. This is a great spot to clear our minds and talk about stuff."

"And people," Ashley added.

"And people," Nathan confirmed.

Will was struck with awe from Fate's Hill. Nathan was right. This place filled Will with tranquility just from standing against the tree. "This place is…amazing," he said to the other two.

"Isn't it?" Ashley asked. "And even though a lot of people know about it, I think we're the only people that come here."

"There aren't even any initials in hearts carved into the tree. That's how secluded this place is, dude. It's awesome!"

"It really is," Will said. "Thanks for showing this to me, guys."

"You're welcome. Anytime you want to come here, let us know," said Ashley.

"Dudes, it's starting!" Nathan said pointing to the east.

The sky was even darker now; however, it was suddenly lit up by an impressive display of fireworks of all colors coming all the way from the Athletic Complex. For exactly eleven-and-a-half minutes, fireworks lit up the night sky and the celebratory noises inspired by them could be heard all the way from the hill. Will's, Ashley's, and Nathan's eyes were wide open as they looked to the skies and watched the display with awe. Something in Will forced him to look back down to the earth for a moment. That's when he saw her, the vision of April in the white dress, sitting on the ground looking up to the fireworks as well. She briefly turned her head towards Will and greeted him with a warm smile.

The fireworks ended, and once again all that could be seen in the sky were the stars and the full moon that had taken its place among them. "They spared no expense this year," Ashley said. "But it was amazing, nonetheless."

"Yeah, it was," Will added.

Nathan stood up from the tree and dusted his hands clean of the dirt from the ground. "Alright, dudes. This Friday night ain't over yet. I say we hit up the Taco King before the game ends and it gets all jockstrap up in there," he said.

Ashley stood up as well and started to follow Nathan back to where their bikes were stationed. "C'mon, Will," she said to Will who was still sitting against the tree.

Will turned his head back at the two and asked, "Can you two give me just a moment? There's something I have to do."

With a puzzled look, Ashley answered, "Alright. We'll be by the trees when you're ready."

Epilogue

"Hello, April. First of all, I want to apologize. I'm sorry that I didn't believe you at first. I didn't think that there was a person in this world who actually wanted to be friends with me. And even now, I still don't think I would've accepted your friendship at first. But you were always there for me regardless, and I appreciate that now.

"I still wish that what happened to you didn't. A lot of times, I wished I could turn back the hands of time and trade my life for yours. For as much as you tried to convince me that I'm destined to live a great life, I saw that in you as well. You were a beacon of hope in a sea of despair, something I couldn't see in many others. It's not fair that you couldn't go on to be an amazing person, to bring that light to so many others as you tried to do with me. But when God calls you home, I suppose you have to go.

"I haven't forgotten our promise, and I never will. From here on out, I will learn to live, to seek out new people and experiences, to not let fear and my own insecurities hinder me from doing so. And in a way, thanks to you, I've found two great friends, who I know will help me fulfill the promise I made to you. I see a lot of you in the both of them. So I'm not going to wait until it's too late to realize what I have before me now as I did before.

"This is the part where I would say goodbye, but I'm not going to. Because even though you're looking down at me from Heaven, I know you're still also here with me in my heart. And I know you'll always be there beside me."

Will got up from the tree and joined his friends waiting for him by the entrance to the woods. He didn't think that the two were in earshot of the conversation he just had, but it wouldn't have mattered anyway. With a smile on his face that surprised both Nathan and Ashley, Will said to the two, "Okay, let's go."

THE END